Do You Know the Monkey Man?

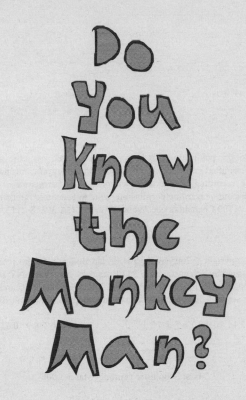

Do You Know the Monkey Man?

DORI HILLESTAD BUTLER

SCHOLASTIC INC.

New York Toronto London Auckland Sydney
Mexico City New Delhi Hong Kong Buenos Aires

ISBN 0-439-86260-4

Text copyright © 2005 by Dori Hillestad Butler. All rights reserved.
Published by Scholastic Inc., 557 Broadway, New York, NY 10012,
by arrangement with Peachtree Publishers, Ltd. SCHOLASTIC and associated
logos are trademarks and/or registered trademarks of Scholastic Inc.

12 11 10 9 8 7 6 5 4 3 2 1   6 7 8 9 10 11/0

Printed in the U.S.A.   40

First Scholastic printing, March 2006

Book design by Melanie McMahon Ives

For my friend, Paula, who was there when I first started thinking about this book…at age thirteen. (See? I always told you I'd dedicate a book to you one day. And I know you always believed I'd do it.)

Acknowledgments

While the act of writing is a solitary activity, no book is ever truly written alone. I'd like to thank Doug Vance of the Coralville Police Department for talking with me about the situation described in this book and for allowing me to interrupt his day on several occasions to ask "just more more question;" Judge E. W. Hertz for patiently and thoroughly answering all my questions on family law; Mary Scarborough for putting me in touch with Mr. Hertz in the first place; my Sisters in Ink friends for letting me ramble on about this project two years in a row; my editor, Lisa Banim, for guiding me in the right direction; and all the people at Peachtree who helped make this book a reality. I'd also like to thank my wonderful husband and children, who give me time and space to write every day…and without whom I wouldn't be who I am today.

—*DHB*

Chapter One

I'm dying here, Sam," my best friend Angela panted as we started up another hill. "Where *is* this place?"

I wasn't enjoying the long bike ride any more than Angela was. It was so hot out it felt like we were biking inside an oven. My shirt was soaked with sweat, my butt was numb, my legs were ready to fall off, and let's not even mention my hair. But I shifted to an easier gear on my bike, wiped my sweaty forehead against my arm, and said, "It's got to be around here somewhere. Let's keep going."

"I don't know, Sam." Angela stopped her bike. "This doesn't look right."

"The ad in the Yellow Pages said North Star Road," I said. "This is North Star Road." But Angela had a point. The houses were pretty spread out around here. There were no businesses anywhere in sight. North Star Road would turn into Highway 1 up ahead and when it did we wouldn't even be in Clearwater anymore. We'd be out in the country.

I glanced around, searching desperately for some clue— *any* clue—that we were headed in the right direction. I noticed a sign in the yard up ahead. Could that be the place?

"Sam!" Angela yelled. "Where are you going?"

I just kept pedaling until I could read the sign. The paint on it was peeling, but I could still make out the black-and-white drawing of a lady gazing into a crystal ball and the words "Psychic Readings by Madame Madeline."

Yes! "This is it!" I cried.

Angela pulled up beside me. She glanced at the house behind the sign and curled her lip in disgust. "You've got to be kidding," she said.

Okay, the house did sort of look like the Bates house in *Psycho*. And like the sign out front, it hadn't been painted in a very long time. Four rotted steps led to a rickety front porch. There was even a window boarded over upstairs.

"I don't know about this," Angela said slowly.

I had to admit I wasn't entirely sure myself. I mean, I'd never been to a real, live psychic before. I didn't even know for sure that Madame Madeline *was* a real psychic. Let's face it, most psychics are fakes. But there are some people out there who really do have some psychic abilities. People who help the police solve crimes or whatever. I had no idea whether Madame Madeline ever did anything like that, but she was the only psychic listed in the Clearwater, Iowa, phone book, so she was my only hope.

"You don't have to come with me if you don't want to," I told Angela as I wheeled my bike over to a lamppost.

"No, no," Angela said, trailing along behind me. "I said I'd go with you and I will. I mean, if you're sure you want to do this. I just think there has to be a better way of finding out where your dad is than going to a psychic."

"Like what?" I asked. My mom was no help. She hated my dad. She got all bent out of shape anytime I even brought him up in conversation.

There were no relatives on his side of the family to ask. Or if there were, I'd never met them. I know my dad grew up in Clearwater, though. I asked some of the older people in my neighborhood if they remembered him. Everybody did ("Such a shame, what happened," Mrs. Inger tsk-tsked.), but nobody seemed to have any idea where he was.

Mrs. Sandvick told me she used to play cards with my dad's mom, which proved I had a Grandma Wright out there somewhere. That made me wonder whether I had any aunts, uncles, or cousins on my dad's side. Mrs. Sandvick couldn't remember whether my dad had any brothers and sisters, but she did remember that Eva Wright always cheated at cards and she was glad that Eva moved away. Then she wanted to know why I was asking so many questions. I was afraid she'd tell my mom I'd been nosing around, so I took my search elsewhere. To the Clearwater Public Library.

There's a sign by the reference desk that says if they don't know the answer to your question, they'll find it. But when I talked to a reference librarian, the woman just sort of pinched her lips together and said they don't get involved in family affairs.

I even tried to find my dad on the Internet. I tried Internet phone books, people finders that didn't cost anything, and basic search engines. But do you have any idea how many Joseph Wrights there are in the world? Millions! I had no idea how to figure out which Joseph Wright was my dad.

How else was I supposed to find him when he'd totally disappeared off the face of the earth?

"I guess I don't have any other bright ideas," Angela said.

"Well, we may as well try Madame Madeline," I said. We locked our bikes to the lamppost and started up the front walk. I wished I had a comb. I had to settle for running my fingers through my hair to untangle it and pouf it up a bit. But it was so humid out, it probably didn't do much good.

"So should we ring the bell or will Madame Madeline just sort of sense that we're here and open the door herself?" Angela muttered.

Before we even reached the first step, Madame Madeline did open the front door. Or somebody did, anyway.

Angela and I stopped where we were and gawked at the woman who stood on the porch. I don't know what I thought a real psychic should look like, but this woman was definitely not it. She looked...well, like a regular person. She wore a yellow sundress like the ones they sell at Wal-Mart with matching flip-flops. She had wavy reddish blond hair that hung to her waist. She was pretty, but if you asked me, she could've used a little eye makeup or blush, something to give her face some color and hide her freckles.

"Do you girls want something?" She looked down at us curiously.

I glanced at Angela, then took a step toward Madeline. "Um, we were wondering," I began. I didn't know how to talk to a psychic. Did I even have to talk, or could she read my mind?

"I mean…" I stammered. "I…uh, saw your ad in the phone book, and, well—"

"Are you Madame Madeline?" Angela blurted out. One thing about Angela, she never has any trouble saying things straight out.

The woman leaned against the cracked doorjamb. "Yes, I am. What can I do for you?"

I cleared my throat. "There's something I have to know," I said, my heart thumping. "I'd like to have a—whatever you call it—a psychic reading?"

At first Madame Madeline didn't say anything. She just inspected me from head to toe. It was kind of unnerving, if you want to know the truth.

"You really are psychic, right?" I had to ask.

She smiled. But instead of answering my question, she said, "Generally I do readings by appointment only."

Appointment? I groaned to myself. Did that mean we'd just biked all the way out here in the blazing hot sun for nothing?

Madame Madeline checked her watch. "But I have a few minutes. Why don't you come in?" She held the door open and a black-and-white cat nuzzled her leg.

Angela raised her eyebrow at me. This was my chance

to change my mind. But no. I had to do this. So we stepped inside.

The cat meowed at us, then turned and padded up the stairs.

I have to say, the inside of the house looked a lot better than the outside. I expected it to be all dark and dreary with long strings of beads hanging in the doorways. But this place was bright and cheerful. No beads. Sunlight poured in through two tall living room windows. And everywhere you looked there were plants—on tables, bookshelves, the windowsills, and the floor.

"I usually give readings in here." Madame Madeline led the way to a small dining room, then turned to look at us. "So who's going to go first?"

"Oh, I'm not doing this." Angela shook her head and backed away. "Just her." She jabbed her thumb at me.

"Then you can have a seat over there." Madame Madeline directed Angela toward an overstuffed chair in the living room. "And you—what's your name?" she asked me.

"Sam," I answered.

"Sam? Is that short for Samantha?"

I nodded.

"Hmm," she said, her index finger tapping against her chin. "I believe that is an old Aramaic name. It means 'listener.'"

I could hear Angela snorting in the other room, but I pretended I didn't. "I don't know," I said to Madame Madeline with a nervous smile.

"Okay, well, why don't you join me here at the table?"

She pulled out a tall, straight-back wooden chair for me. I slowly eased myself down. Madame Madeline sat beside me.

"So the reason I'm here—" I began.

"Shh!" She put her finger to her lips. "May I see your hand?"

I held out my hand. I figured she was going to read my palm or something, but she was more interested in the back of my hand than my palm. She traced her finger over the big vein that stuck out. It tickled a little.

I glanced over my shoulder at Angela. She was trying really hard not to laugh. I shouldn't have asked her to come with me. I was serious about this.

I turned back to Madame Madeline. "Don't you want to know why I'm here?" I asked impatiently, my foot tapping against my chair.

"I know why you're here," she replied. She still had hold of my hand. "You have questions. Many questions. And these questions cannot be answered through normal channels."

"Um...yeah." Something like that.

"I can't guarantee a specific answer to your questions," Madame Madeline said. "All I can do is tell you what I see. The answers to your questions may be there or they may not. Do you understand?"

I nodded.

"Do you wish to continue?"

"Sure," I said.

"Then my fee is twenty-five dollars. Payable up front, please."

"Oh." I blinked. "Okay." I unzipped my purse, pulled out a wad of hard-earned baby-sitting money, and counted out twenty-five bucks. If Madame Madeline could really tell me where my dad was, she'd be worth every penny.

Madame Madeline stuffed the bills into the pocket of her sundress, then peered into my eyes. I felt like she could see all the way through to my soul.

Finally she spoke. "You're a bright girl, Sam. You do fine in school."

"I guess that depends on your definition of 'fine,'" I mumbled. I got mostly B's in school. Sometimes I got a C in math or gym. In my mom's book, C's were practically failing.

"And you have friends," Madame Madeline went on.

Friends? Yes. Popularity? No.

"It isn't school or your social life that brings you here today. It's something else." Madame Madeline picked up my hand again and turned it around. "It's your family. Something about your family is out of balance. Something troubles you very deeply."

"Yes!" I leaned toward her eagerly.

"Your family is divided. There are two on one side and two on the other."

I didn't quite know what she meant by that. "There are only two people in my family," I said. "Just me and my mom. Unless you count Bob. My mom and Bob are getting married pretty soon."

"Bob is your mother's fiancé?" Madame Madeline asked.

I nodded. "Yes."

Madame Madeline frowned. "I do feel that connection. But there's another connection, too. A deeper one. Another man has been important to your mother. And another child, too. Was your mother married before? Do you, perhaps, have a sister?"

My jaw dropped. How did she know that? "I *had* a sister," I admitted. "She died."

Madame Madeline looked confused. "Then there must be another one. Another child that your mother is connected to. And you, too. I feel these connections very strongly. There's something that separates this child from you, but it isn't death. This connection is so strong that the other child must be alive."

I shook my head. "Sarah died when we were three. We were twins."

"Ah, twins. That's why the connection is so strong."

"Could we please talk about my dad?" I asked. "I haven't heard from him since I was, like, six years old and well, that's sort of why I'm here—"

"I need to hear more about your sister," Madame Madeline interrupted. "Would you mind telling me how she died?"

"She drowned."

"I don't think so." Madeline frowned again.

I blinked in surprise. "Yes, she did. I remember."

"You were there?"

"Well, no. But I remember."

Madame Madeline shook her head. "I don't think you do. And I don't think your sister is dead, Samantha. I think she's very much alive."

Chapter Two

Well, that was bizarre," Angela said as we coasted down the hill on our bikes, our hair flying out behind us. "What a nutcase!"

"Yeah, I guess," I said. I knew Sarah couldn't be alive. She drowned in the old quarry when we were three. That was ten years ago. But what a weird thing for Madame Madeline to tell me. How did she even know I'd had a sister?

"Why would she tell you your sister's alive?" Angela went on. "That just seems mean."

"I don't think she meant to be mean," I said, braking as we got near the intersection at the bottom of the hill. "I think she just, I don't know, got her signals crossed or something."

The light was green, so we continued on through the intersection. "What signals?" Angela snorted. "That woman was about as psychic as I am. You should get your money back."

I had to admit Angela was probably right. And I shouldn't have been surprised. I mean, you couldn't expect a real live psychic to live in Clearwater, Iowa. Still, I couldn't help feeling disappointed. Madame Madeline was my last hope for finding my dad. And she hadn't said a word about him. Not one word.

Angela and I turned onto Center Street. We had to ride single file now, because there was a lot more traffic. As I pedaled, I thought about my dad.

It had been so long since I'd seen him that I could hardly picture him anymore. I knew he was tall and thin and he had hair that was so blond it was practically white. Just like mine. But I couldn't see him in my mind at all.

There were no pictures of him around our house. No nothing of him around our house. All I had left of him was a crumpled-up postcard with a monkey on it that he mailed from the San Diego Zoo when I was six. The note on the back read, "For my Sammy Bear. With love from the Monkey Man."

I didn't know for sure why my mom and dad got divorced. My mom told me a long time ago that it was because my dad was irresponsible and childish. But once when Grandma Sperling was visiting from Florida, she told me my mom and dad never had a good marriage. She said they got married really young and then when Sarah died, their whole marriage fell apart. She also said that the death of a child is the worst thing that can happen to a couple and that lots of people get divorced afterwards.

Angela and I moved to the sidewalk because now there was even more traffic and the road was pretty narrow. The sidewalk was even narrower, though.

I could sort of remember the day Sarah died. My mom would say I couldn't possibly remember that, but I did. It was a day a lot like today, really hot and sticky. My mom and dad and Sarah and I were going to go on a picnic. But I was sick, so I couldn't go. I also remembered Mom and Dad fighting that day. Fighting about me. Dad thought I was well enough to go on the picnic. But Mom said no. In the end, she stayed home with me while Dad and Sarah went to the old Clearwater quarry.

Dad took her out on the water in his canoe. I know he shouldn't have done that. You're not supposed to go swimming or boating in the quarry. But he did it anyway. And somehow the canoe tipped over and my dad and Sarah fell into the water. My dad tried to save her, but he couldn't.

I don't know what happened after that. I just know that one day my dad went away and he never came back.

Now my mom's getting married again. I can deal with that. Really, I can. The only problem is, they want Bob to adopt me. And I'm not sure I want him to.

What about my real dad? Doesn't he have to give permission or anything?

Mom says he doesn't because he's been gone so long. Nobody knows where he is. Mom says we can do whatever we want because he gave up parenting rights a long time ago.

Well, nobody ever asked me what *I* want. I want to find my dad. I want to know what he thinks about some other guy adopting me.

"You look pretty serious," Angela said, riding up beside

me. We had turned onto McGregor, which was a quiet, tree-lined residential street, so we were back in the road. I hadn't even realized it.

"What are you thinking about?" Angela asked.

I shrugged. I wasn't much in the mood for talking.

"You still disappointed that that psychic couldn't help you find your father?" Angela pressed.

"Sort of."

"You know, Sam…" I could tell Angela was about to say something I wasn't going to like. "Maybe you should just forget about your dad and let Bob adopt you."

Let Bob adopt me? She had to be kidding!

"At least he's nice. And I bet he really wants to adopt you. He's not just doing it for your mom."

"But he's not my dad. And I don't want a piece of paper that says he is when he isn't. I've got a real dad out there somewhere."

"Real fathers are overrated, Sam," Angela said. "Look at mine."

Angela's dad wouldn't win any Father of the Year awards, but at least he was part of her life. Sort of. He sent birthday and Christmas gifts. She and her older brother even visited him in Minnesota sometimes. Well, okay, they hadn't visited in a while. But that was because Mr. Hunter and his wife had a baby last year.

"At least you know your dad," I said.

"Father," Angela corrected. "Not dad. And yeah, I know him." Her bike wobbled a little when she said that. "I know he ran off with some other woman, got married, and had

13

another kid who is tons more important to him than Andrew and I are. He's a selfish jerk. That's what I know about him."

"You know more than that," I pointed out. "You know whether you look like him or talk like him. You know which habits and personality quirks you got from him. You know what he does for a living, what he does in his spare time, what he eats for breakfast. I don't know any of that about my dad."

Angela snorted. "I still say you're better off."

"How?" How could a person *ever* be better off not knowing their dad?

"Because right now, your father could be anyone. Anyone you want him to be. But once you find him, that's it. There's no more pretending. You're stuck with whoever he is."

"That's okay," I insisted. "I don't care who he is. He's my dad. That's all that matters."

"That's easy for you to say now when you don't know anything about him. Don't get your hopes up. That's all I'm saying."

I looked away. Sometimes Angela's kind of negative. It's easier for her that way. But me, I try to look on the bright side. I mean, if you don't have hope, what do you have?

* * *

There's a For Sale sign in front of our little blue house on Hartman Lane. My mom and Bob are building a bigger house in one of the new developments, so we're moving after the wedding.

I'll be closer to Angela when we move. I'll have a bigger room with built-in bookshelves, a built-in window seat, and my own bathroom. But I'd still rather stay here. This is my house, you know? It's the only place I've ever lived.

Besides, if my dad ever came looking for me, this is where he'd come. This is where we lived when my parents were married. If I had a new name and a new house, he wouldn't know where to look for me.

I fumbled around in my purse for my house key, then unlocked the front door. Right away my cat padded over to me and meowed.

"Hey, Sherlock," I said, bending to pick him up. The motorboat in his gut revved up as I buried my face in his fur. My cat has the loudest purr of any cat I've ever heard. But I'm not complaining. When cats purr, they're telling you they love you.

I set Sherlock down on the floor and he followed me down the hall. One whole wall in our hallway is lined with pictures. Pictures of me, pictures of Mom, pictures of me and Mom, pictures of me and Mom and Grandma and Grandpa Sperling. But the other wall only has two pictures on it—an 8 x 10 of my eighth-grade school picture and an 8 x 10 of Sarah from when we were three.

There were other pictures of Sarah in albums somewhere, but this was the only big one we had of her. And it was the only one that was out where people could see it. She's got on a frilly white dress with a matching ribbon in her hair. She looks kind of shy because she's not smiling very big and she's got her hands folded neatly in her lap.

Somewhere there was a picture of me that looked almost the same (like I said, we were twins), except I was wearing a frilly blue dress instead of a frilly white dress. At one time, that picture probably hung right next to the picture of Sarah. But Mom puts up my new school picture every year. Sarah's picture always stays the same.

Why was I still obsessing about my sister? There was no way she could still be alive. She's out at Lakeview Cemetery right by the big oak tree. End of story.

I headed to my room. Man, was I tired after all that biking. As I flopped down on my bed, I caught a glimpse of my hair in the mirror. It looked like someone had taken a mixer to it. I reached for my brush and immediately went to work.

Sherlock jumped up beside me and meowed. He turned around a couple times, then settled down right next to my favorite stuffed monkey. It's just an old, floppy brown thing. I don't even know where I got it. But it seems like I've always had it. I tickled Sherlock under the chin with the monkey's tail and he purred. Silly cat.

Then I went back to my hair. I'm not sure whether the trip to the psychic was worth this much damage. I don't even know what I was thinking going to see a psychic in the first place. About all I can say about it is it worked in *Who Is Victor Marsh?* which is a really good book that I read last week. It was about a woman who was looking for her long-lost brother. The police were looking for him, too, because they thought he was a serial killer. But the woman thought they were wrong. She wanted to find her brother before the police did, so she hired this psychic. The psychic not only found the brother, she also found the real killer.

I love books like that. I love all books, but I especially love mysteries. In fact, I think I'd like to be a mystery writer when I grow up.

My mom says I'm dreaming if I think I can make a living as a writer. She loves to say stuff like that. She can be just as negative as Angela sometimes. I once asked her what was so bad about having dreams and she said, "You can't live on them." Maybe not, but I still think dreams are important.

Slam!

Speak of the devil.

"Hello?" my mom called out. "Sam? Are you home?"

"Yeah," I called back. I put the finishing touches on my hair, then took a quick glance around my room. There wasn't much she could complain about. A few books on the floor. And my nightshirt. I stacked the books on my desk next to my flute case and kicked the nightshirt under my bed.

"Sam!" Mom yelled again from the main part of the house.

"What?" I trotted down to the kitchen.

Mom stood by the sink with her hands on her hips. She had on her nurse's uniform—white pants, a pastel blue flowery shirt, and white shoes. She looked tired. "Why are the breakfast dishes still sitting in the sink?" she asked.

Oops. "Um, I guess I didn't get around to putting them in the dishwasher," I said.

"Why not?"

I shrugged.

"What did you do all day?" She frowned at the pile of empty boxes that were still stacked up in the corner. She had asked me to start boxing up stuff that we weren't likely to need in the next month, but well…I didn't get to that either.

What could I say? I just shrugged again.

Mom sighed. "Could you at least take care of the dishes before we go?"

"Go?" Where were we going?

"Today's Bob's mother's birthday," Mom said, as though I should have known. "They're having a big party at her house tonight. Everyone's going to be there."

Everyone, of course, meant Bob's brother and sisters and all their husbands and wives and small children.

I tried not to groan. "Do I have to go?"

"You don't want to?" She sounded shocked.

"Well, it's just that…" I began. It's just that I feel weird around Bob's family. I don't mean they're horrible people. They're okay. But there are so many of them. And they're all so loud and so…I don't know. Just *different* from me.

"It's just that what?" Mom asked.

I kicked at a crumb on the floor. "Nothing. It's fine. I'll go." It wasn't like she'd let me stay home anyway.

"We'll leave in about an hour," Mom said. "Please try to look presentable."

"So I should leave my nose ring at home?" I was joking. I don't have a nose ring. I have earrings. I wear two in one earlobe and one in the other. But no nose ring, eyebrow ring, tongue ring, belly button ring—nothing like that.

I honestly thought I was being funny. But Mom just walked away, shaking her head.

See, that's the thing about me and my mom. We just don't understand each other. We haven't for a long time.

I think the problem is I'm not turning into the person she wants me to be. I'm a person with dreams. She wants me to be a person with "goals." Dreams and goals are not the same thing.

Maybe that was why I wanted to find my dad so bad. I had a feeling I wouldn't ever have to explain things to him. He'd just understand.

Chapter Three

Bob's mother lives in the Lyndhurst neighborhood. That's the really old, nice neighborhood near downtown. The houses are big and close together. And the trees are so tall and thick they practically form an umbrella over the whole street.

There were so many cars in front of Bob's mother's house that we had to drive around the corner to park. Mom found a spot in front of a police car. It probably belonged to one of Bob's brothers. Just about everyone in his family is a cop. Bob's dad was a cop, too. But he got killed during a robbery or something a long time ago.

Before we got out of the car, Mom put her hand on my arm. "Please try and have a good time, Sam," she said. "In another month, these people are going to be family."

They're going to be *her* family, not mine. But I just said, "Sure." Whatever.

I tucked in my blouse and smoothed my skirt while Mom carefully picked up the gift-wrapped square box from the back seat. Then I grabbed the mystery I'd been reading and the birthday card I'd whipped up in about ten minutes on our computer before we left, and we trudged back to Bob's mother's house. As soon as we started up the walk, Bob came out onto the porch.

My mom's whole face lit up when she saw him. I have to tell you, for a middle-aged guy, Bob's not bad looking. He's got brown hair like my mom's, blue eyes, and a really nice smile that makes you smile back whether you mean to or not.

Bob's nothing like the cops you see on TV. He's kind of quiet. I can't imagine him ever pulling a gun on anyone and yelling, "Stop! You're under arrest!"

"Hi, hon." Bob bent down and hugged my mom. He glanced at me over her shoulder. "Sam, how are you?"

"Okay."

"*Suzanne!*" Bob's mother bellowed as she came to the door. She's almost a whole head shorter than I am, but you'd never know it by her voice. People halfway down the block could probably hear her.

My Grandma Sperling is totally different from Bob's mom. She's more quiet and reserved. And she wears polyester pantsuits all the time, even when she's just sitting around the condo. Bob's mother wears stained T-shirts that say "If Mom Says No, Ask Grandma." It kind of makes me wonder how these two ladies are going to get along when Grandma and Grandpa Sperling come for the wedding in a few weeks.

"I'm so glad you could come," Bob's mom said, reaching up to hug my mom.

"Me, too." My mom hugged her back. "Happy birthday, Mom."

Mom? When did she start calling Bob's mother Mom?

"And Samantha!" I tried not to stiffen when Bob's mother reached out to hug me. "It's nice to see you again."

Bob's mother told me a long time ago that I should call her Grandma. But I don't think of her as Grandma. I think of her as "Bob's mother." I don't want to hurt her feelings, though, so I just avoid the whole issue by not calling her anything.

I pasted a cheery smile on my face. "Happy birthday," I said, handing her my card. I held tight to my book with my elbow.

"Thank you, sweetie. You didn't have to make me a card."

Well, yes, actually, I did, but whatever.

I followed my mom into the living room. Something smelled good. Lasagna, I think. One thing I could say for this party, we'd be eating well. The people in Bob's family are excellent cooks.

We don't do a lot of fancy cooking in our family. Mom never makes anything that requires more than ten minutes of work. I'm not sure my grandparents even know how to cook. We always eat out when we're with them.

Mom and I wound our way around all the TV trays and toys that were scattered around the living room. There was a bunch of ladies standing around talking and laughing in the kitchen. All the men except Bob and all the little kids (the next oldest kid after me is about seven) were running around out in the backyard.

"Hey, everyone!" Bob's mother announced. "Look who's here." As soon as Bob's sisters and sisters-in-law saw my mom, the hugging started all over again. They're really big on hugging in this family.

I hung back in the living room. My mom looked so happy. So comfortable. Like she was already one of them. Me, I couldn't imagine ever being one of them.

"I see Rick's kids are playing ball out back." Bob touched my arm. "Do you want to go out?"

Bob's really trying here. I know that. He wants us all to be one big, happy family, just like my mom does. But no matter how hard we both try, he and his family are not my family. And going out in the backyard to play with a plastic ball and bat and run around some trees with all those little kids isn't going to change that.

"Thanks," I said, holding up my book. "But I think maybe I'll just stay in here and read."

"All by yourself?"

I doubted anybody in this family ever did anything by themselves. None them were readers, either.

I shrugged. "I like to read." Besides, it was kind of hard to play in a skirt.

"Okay," Bob said, sounding really disappointed. "But come and join us if you change your mind."

As soon as he left, I plopped down on the couch. It was one of those poufy couches with lots of pillows that you sort of sink into. I love couches like this. I pulled my feet up under me and opened my book. But I'd barely read two pages before my mom burst into the room. Bob's mother and all his sisters and sisters-in-law were right behind her, all smiles and excitement.

"Guess what, Sam!" Mom said. Her face glowed. "Bob's mother finished your bridesmaid's dress!"

"She did?"

"Why don't you come try it on so we can see how it fits?" Bob's mother said.

"Okay." I had to admit I was curious about this dress. And I'm always up for trying on clothes. Who wouldn't be? So I set my book down and followed everyone up to Bob's mother's bedroom. I had to dodge a bunch of Matchbox cars and Beanie Babies along the way. Geez, you'd think ten kids lived here instead of one lady.

"Oh my goodness!" Mom clasped her hands to her cheeks when she saw the blue dress that hung on a hanger over the back of the bedroom door. Everyone else oohed and aahed, too.

I was pretty amazed myself. I'd seen the shiny blue taffeta fabric my mom had picked out. And I'd seen the dress pattern. But seeing the whole thing together for the first time... Wow! I didn't know what to say.

"Do you like it?" Mom asked me.

"Oh, yeah. Definitely." Mom and I hardly ever have the same taste in clothes, but I did like this dress. It was simple, but elegant. There was no lace, just the smooth taffeta. You could wear it on the shoulders or off, but if I knew my mom, I'd be wearing it up.

Bob's mother carefully took the dress down from the hanger. "Let's see how it looks on you," she said, holding it out to me.

She didn't expect me to actually get undressed in front

of all these people, did she? I didn't mind my mom being there, but I don't like to undress in front of strangers.

"You did a great job on this, Mom," one of the sisters or sisters-in-law said as she ran her finger along the smooth skirt.

"You sure did," my mom agreed. She unzipped the dress. "Come on, Sam," she said impatiently. "Try it on."

Apparently no one was leaving. I kicked my shoes off, slid my skirt down, and unbuttoned my blouse. Unfortunately, I wasn't wearing a strapless bra, so I had to take my regular old bra off. I tried to cover up a little.

Mom sighed. "Move your arms, Sam. How are we going to get a dress on when your arms are crossed?"

I moved my arms. Then my mom and Bob's mother carefully eased the dress over my head. It made kind of a crinkly, swishy sound as it dropped into place. I reached back to lift my hair, then looked down. The dress hung all the way to the floor.

"Oh, Sam." My mom had tears in her eyes.

I turned to look at myself in the mirror and my eyeballs nearly popped out of my head. I looked so *different*. Older, definitely. But sort of mature, too. Like I'd had all these huge life experiences or something.

Mom gathered my hair and held it on top of my head. "Here. You hold your hair and I'll zip you up," she said.

The dress tightened around my chest as the zipper went up.

"You look…" Mom stopped. She was at a loss for words.

"She looks absolutely breathtaking," Bob's mother said.

Breathtaking? Me?

"Yes, she does," the sisters-in-law all agreed.

Bob's mother had me climb up on a chair so she could pin the hem. Then they all started talking about what a beautiful wedding it was going to be and how nice it was that Grandpa Sperling was coming all the way from Florida to walk Mom down the aisle.

Even though it was a second marriage for my mom, it was a first marriage for Bob, so they were going all out on the ceremony. My mom says that maybe if she does the wedding up right this time, maybe the marriage will work out better.

I do hope the marriage works out. Really, I do. I want my mom to be happy. But…I want to be happy, too. Is that so wrong? And the one thing that could really, truly make me happy would be finding my dad.

Chapter Four

On Thursday morning I finished the book I was reading, fixed my hair, practiced my flute, and then, because it was too stormy outside to do anything else, I actually did what my mom wanted me to do. I took a bunch of empty boxes down to our dingy old laundry/storage room in the basement and started boxing up stuff that we probably wouldn't need until after we moved. The blender. The Crock-Pot. Extra Tupperware. I hoped my mom wouldn't decide two days from now that she needed some of this stuff after all. But at least she couldn't complain that I never made any effort around here.

I hated this room. It was dark and gloomy. The only light came from a single lightbulb that hung from the ceiling in the middle of the room. The whole place smelled like old, wet rags. Probably because the only "carpet" down here was a big rug that really was made from old rags. I think it was my grandma's. Plus there were spiders. Tons of them.

I could hear the low rumble of thunder and the *plink plink plink* of rain against the little window above my head.

The bulb flickered, but it didn't go out. So I kept working.

Once I cleared the shelves by the washer and dryer, I moved on to the ones across from the deep freeze. Most of this stuff was already boxed up. I probably didn't have to do anything with it, but I pulled out one of the boxes and peeked inside just to see what was there. The whole box was full of old Barbie stuff.

I smiled. I used to love Barbies. Playing Barbies was one of the few things I remembered doing with my sister. In fact, I could even remember my mom getting down on the floor and playing with us, too. She was fun then. We'd dress all the Barbies in fancy clothes, then send them to Cinderella's ball. Wow. I had no idea my mom, Ms. Let's-Go-Through-the-House-and-Get-Rid-of-Stuff, saved all this. Who knew what else was down here?

I shoved that box back where I found it and pulled out another. This one was a lot heavier. I had to pull hard to get it out. When I opened it up, I discovered it was full of old Dr. Seuss books. *The Cat in the Hat. Hop on Pop. Green Eggs and Ham.*

There were more boxes way in the back. Unlike the ones in front, these were all sealed up with several layers of strong packing tape. I ran upstairs to get a sharp knife, then came back down. There was so much tape on the one box, it was hard to cut through. But eventually I got through it all and yanked open the flaps. Inside were a few ribbons that belonged to my mother, a dried corsage, and an old Clearwater High School yearbook.

Well, this could be interesting. I pulled out the yearbook and looked up Suzanne Sperling in the index. I wondered how dorky my mom looked in high school. It turned out she looked pretty much the same as she does now. Same hairstyle and everything. My mom was in band, yearbook, cross country (my mom ran cross country?), and Future Scientists of America. That last one was even more surprising than the cross country.

My mom and dad graduated from high school together, I knew. They were in the same class, even though Dad was a year older. With trembling fingers I flipped ahead to the W's. But there was no Joseph Wright listed. The W's went from Terry Warner to David Wyatt. After all the senior portraits, there was a list of students not pictured: Michelle Mallory, Samuel Roth, and Joseph Wright. Why was I not surprised? I wasn't sure I'd ever seen a photo of my dad.

I started packing everything back into the box when I realized I'd almost missed a small black velvet box like the kind you get from a jewelry store. I opened it up and just about choked. Inside was a ring. A *wedding* ring. At least, I was pretty sure it was a wedding ring. It had a simple gold band with a diamond sticking up. Was this the ring my mom wore when she and my dad were married?

I was about to lift the ring out of the velvet casing and take a closer look when...*ding dong!* The sound of the door-bell startled me so much I nearly dropped the ring. I set the box down, then scurried up the stairs two at a time.

I opened the front door and found Angela standing on my front porch. She had on a soaking wet yellow raincoat. Her hair hung in wet curls around her shoulders.

"Hey," I said, opening the screen door to let her in.

"Hey yourself." She stomped her feet on the doormat and water splattered all over my feet. "Get your shoes and coat. It's a great day to go to the mall!"

I stared at the sheets of rain pounding the driveway. "You've got to be kidding. You want to go to the mall now?" Both our moms were working, so there was no one to drive us. We'd have to walk. In the pouring rain.

"Why not?" She grinned. "Ben Willard might be there."

I could feel my face heating up. Ben Willard is hot. He used to have this thick curly hair, but all the jocks got buzz cuts for the summer. Ben and his friends hung out at Tilt, which was this place at the mall with video games and skee-ball. But it wasn't like they ever noticed us. And to tell you the truth, I wasn't sure I wanted to them to notice us after we'd just walked a mile and a half in the pouring rain.

"I don't know," I said. "I'm kind of busy."

"Busy? Doing what?"

"Come on. I'll show you."

Angela slipped off her raincoat, kicked off her shoes, then followed me downstairs.

I showed her the ring. She took it out of the box and held it up to the light to inspect it. "Nice."

"I think it's my mom's old wedding ring."

"Really?" Angela squinted at the inside. "Is it engraved?"

"I don't know," I said. "I just found it before you got here." I peered all around the inside of the gold band, but I didn't see any engraving.

"My mom's ring says, 'Always, Tom.'" Angela snorted. "What a joke!"

"I should put it back," I said, taking the ring back from Angela. I put the velvet box back inside the big cardboard box and looked around for some tape to seal it back up.

"You found a diamond ring packed away in an old box down here?" Angela asked.

"Yup," I said. Unfortunately, I couldn't find any tape, so I just folded the flaps under one another and slid the box back onto the shelf.

"My mom doesn't wear her old wedding ring, either," Angela said as she slowly lowered herself to the floor. "But she keeps it in a dresser drawer. Not in a box in the basement."

"Well, I'm surprised my mom kept her ring at all. She got rid of everything else that had to do with my dad. Pictures. Videos. Everything."

"Everything?" Angela asked, wide-eyed.

"Everything."

"Wow, she must really hate him."

"Yeah," I said. "I guess so."

Angela leaned back against the washer and stretched her legs out in front of her. "So what are you going to do if you actually find your dad?" she asked.

I pulled out another box. "What do you mean?"

"Well, what will you tell your mom? I can't imagine she'll just smile and say 'Oh, how nice for you.' Do you think she'll even let you see him?"

I had to admit, I hadn't thought about that.

"I don't know," I said, resting my elbows on the box. "Maybe I won't tell her. Maybe I'll just go run away and live with him."

"What?" Angela cried. "You don't even *know* him. What makes you think you'd want to live with him?"

I shrugged. "He's my dad. Why wouldn't I want to live with him? I doubt my mom would miss me anyway. She's got Bob. I'm old enough to choose, don't you think?"

"I don't know. Doesn't your mom have custody? I don't think you can just decide to go live with your dad."

"You should be able to when you're thirteen," I said as I plunged my knife into the tape on the box in front of me.

Angela crossed her legs. "You know, you've never really told me about your dad," she said. "What do you remember about him?"

"Not much." I lifted the flaps on the box.

"What did he do for a living when he was married to your mom?"

"I don't know. I don't think he worked much."

"Why not?"

"I have no idea. I think he wanted to be a musician." Somebody, I don't remember who, had told me that. "Maybe he was waiting for his big break or something."

"A musician?" Angela raised her eyebrow. "Cool! What did he play?"

"I don't think he played anything. I think he just sang." I smiled. "I remember he used to take all these songs that everybody knows and he'd change the words. Like that muffin man song. He used to sing, 'Do you know the monkey man, the monkey man, the monkey man? Do you know the monkey man, who lives on Hartman Lane?'"

Angela giggled. "Sorry, Sam, but you did *not* inherit your father's musical talent."

I made a face at her. "Hey, I never said I did."

I turned my attention to the box in front of me. I lifted the flaps. A single dried pink rose lay right on top.

Oh. My. Gosh.

I suddenly flashed back to a time when I was a really little kid and I was holding my stuffed monkey and all these grown-ups were milling around crying and...there were pink roses all over the house.

Sarah's funeral.

"What's the matter?" Angela asked.

I couldn't answer her. I felt like the floor had dropped out underneath me. Mom and I didn't talk about my dad very often, but we *never* talked about Sarah.

I set the dried-out flower aside, then checked to see what else was in the box. It looked like old photo albums. I lifted the top album out and opened it up.

"Is that you and your sister?" Angela pointed at a snapshot of two little girls dressed in identical pink dresses standing in front of a white house.

I slid the photo out of the plastic holder to get a closer look. It had to have been taken right before Sarah died. We both looked a lot like that picture of her that hung in our hallway. We had wispy white blond hair that touched our shoulders. Neither of us was smiling. In fact, we both looked a little worried. Like maybe we sensed that something bad was about to happen.

"Which one's you?" Angela asked.

I squinted at first one girl, then the other. "I—I don't know." It felt weird that I couldn't tell. But each girl was an exact copy of the other. It was like someone took a picture of a house, then plopped the same little kid in the picture two times.

"Look. There are some old newspapers in here." Angela reached into the box and pulled out a small stack of newspaper pages that had been folded over and tied with a string.

I slipped the photo into my jeans pocket, then took the stack from Angela. I slid the string off and gasped as I realized what the articles were about.

"These are all about the drowning."

"Let me see." Angela leaned over and we read the first article together. The headline was missing.

CLEARWATER—An afternoon at the old Clearwater quarry turned tragic for a father and daughter last night. Joseph Wright, 21, of Clearwater, told police that he and his daughter Sarah, 3, had been canoeing at the quarry. The canoe capsized and Wright unsuccessfully searched the dark, murky water for his daughter. Jonathan Avery, 35, of Cedar Rapids and his wife Joanne, 32, told police that they were out walking at the quarry and saw someone fall into the water. A child's life preserver was found in the canoe, but so far divers have been unable to recover the body. The water depth in some parts of the quarry can reach up to three hundred feet. "We hope Sarah somehow managed to get to shore and is out there somewhere, waiting to be found," the missing child's mother, Suzanne Wright, said late last night. Ms. Wright also reported that her daughter did not know how to swim. The search for Sarah Wright is expected to resume today.

"Wow," Angela said.

"Yeah. Wow." I felt somehow removed from everything. Like this was an article about some other family instead of my own. That quote didn't even sound like my mom. She sounded...emotional. Emotional is not a word I'd use to describe my mom.

"Here's another one," I said, setting the first article aside.

> —The search continues for three-year-old Sarah Wright of Clearwater. Sarah was last seen on Thursday afternoon at the old Clearwater quarry when the canoe she and her father were in capsized. A crew from Cedar Rapids has been dragging the quarry since Thursday, but according to Capt. Jim Morgan of the Linn County sheriff's office, the search has been unsuccessful. "The truth is, he said, we have no idea where little Sarah's body might be."

That article had a picture of my mom and dad. Finally, an actual photo with my dad in it. I peered hard at the newspaper clipping.

He was young. Which I guess made sense, considering the picture would've been taken ten years ago. My mom looked pretty young in that picture, too.

He was wearing blue jeans and a white undershirt with no other shirt over it. He had really light hair that covered his ears, a thick mustache, and a pointy nose, kind of like mine. I ran my finger across his nose. *Where are you, Dad?* I thought as I looked into his eyes. *And why haven't you been in touch in all these years?*

"What do the other articles say?" Angela asked.

I set that article aside and picked up the next one. It didn't really say anything new. In fact, as I skimmed through the whole pile of articles, I noticed they all sounded the same until we got to Sarah's obituary. Then it was like, this is it. The end. Sarah's really dead. The final line of the obituary really drove the point home. "Sarah is survived by one sister, Samantha, also age 3."

Except…there was something missing. Something that surely should have been mentioned in at least one of these articles…I flipped back through them again, reading each one more thoroughly this time. Had I just missed it before?

"What are you looking for?" Angela asked.

"Shh!" I had to concentrate.

But when I got to the end of the pile, I still hadn't found it.

I looked at Angela. "Did you notice that every one of those articles talked about this big search they were doing for Sarah? Every one of them either begins or ends with, 'the search continues.' But there's nothing in here that says when or where her body was found," I said.

"Maybe it wasn't found?" Angela suggested.

A little chill crept up my back when she said that.

The psychic lady's words came back to me: *I don't think your sister is dead, Samantha. I think she's very much alive.*

"Maybe it wasn't," I said slowly.

Angela looked a little confused.

"What if that psychic was right?" I asked. "What if Sarah's body was never found because she's…not dead?"

"Whoa." Angela's eyes seemed to grow to the size of golf balls.

"I know there's a gravestone out at Lakeside Cemetery, but that doesn't mean there's actually anyone buried there. Grandma and Grandpa Sperling have gravestones. I think you can buy one whenever you want."

Angela opened her mouth to say something, then closed it. When she finally opened it again, she said, "Listen to me, Sam. Nobody buys a gravestone for a little kid unless that little kid is dead."

"Maybe everyone just thinks she's dead, but really she's not?" I suggested.

Angela frowned. "Well, if she's not dead, where do you think she is?"

"I don't know." I flipped through the articles until I came to the first one we'd read. "It says here that maybe she found her way to shore. Maybe somebody found her? Somebody who wasn't from around here. Maybe they took her home and raised her as their own kid?"

Angela wrinkled her nose. "Don't you think that sounds a little Movie of the Week? How would she have gotten to shore? She was three years old. She couldn't swim."

"Maybe she could."

Angela grabbed the article and held it in front of my face. "Your mom said she couldn't. Listen to me, Sam. The old Clearwater quarry is huge. And it's really deep. If your sister's body was never found, it's because there was too much water. Not because she somehow survived."

"You don't know that for sure," I said.

I could tell Angela thought I had gone totally crazy, but

I've read enough detective novels to know that until the detective finds the body, it's almost impossible for the DA to prove murder. That's because without a body, there's still a chance, even a really small one, that the person is actually alive.

Angela cocked her head at me. "Do you honestly believe your sister's still alive, Sam?"

Did I? I looked down at the articles in my lap. "I don't know. It's possible."

"No way." Angela shook her head.

But as far as I was concerned, the only way it *wasn't* possible was if Sarah's body was buried in her gravesite at Lakeview Cemetery. And that was easy enough to find out. All I had to do was ask my mom.

Chapter Five

Look alive out there, Wright!" Coach Frye called as the ball sailed over my head. Softball is not exactly my sport. I'm not sure I have a sport.

I probably should've done my team a favor and not gone out for softball. But Angela really wanted to play again this summer, so I figured I might as well play, too. The thing is, Angela's actually good at softball. But me? I get a hit maybe once every three or four times I'm up at bat, and I can't catch or throw for anything. Just ask Bob. He saw me play a few weeks ago and right afterward, he offered to give me a few pointers. But hey, it's just a game. So what if I'm bad at it?

I scurried after the ball and threw it to our pitcher, Marianna Detert, but it went a little short. Ashley Frye shook her head like she couldn't believe how bad I was. She grabbed the ball and lobbed it underhand to Marianna. By then the runner for the Central City team was already home.

"Sorry," I called out. I'll admit I was even more off than usual today. I just couldn't stop thinking about those newspaper articles. And Sarah. Was I crazy to think there was a chance my sister was still alive?

"Look out, Sam! Fly ball!" Angela shouted.

Before I could react, something whacked me hard in the forehead and knocked me to the ground.

"Sam? Sam? Are you okay?" someone asked. I could feel the ground tremble as everyone stampeded toward me.

I closed my eyes and let my head rest on the ground. My whole head was ringing and it hurt. A lot.

"Sam?" Coach Frye patted my cheek. "Can you hear me, Sam?"

My eyelids fluttered open and I peered into a sea of concerned faces.

"She's not unconscious," Ashley noted.

"No, but she's going to have quite a goose egg in the middle of her forehead," Coach Frye said.

I'm not sure if I groaned out of pain or self pity. Just what I needed. A goose egg in the middle of my forehead.

"Are you okay, Sam?" Coach Frye asked.

"I think so," I said, trying to sit up. I blinked a few times.

"Are you dizzy?" Coach Frye asked.

"I—I don't know." Ow! It felt like someone had closed a waffle iron around my head. I felt for the bump on my forehead. It was already about the size of an egg.

Coach Frye helped me to the bench. Angela brought me an ice pack and Coral Wilson offered me two Tylenol. The girls from the Central City team all stood around like they were bored.

Coach Frye grabbed a cell phone out of his gym bag. "I think we'd better call your mom."

"Okay. Wait…what time is it?" I tried not to moan.

He checked his watch. "About five thirty."

"I…I don't think you'll be able to reach her." I touched my head gently. "She should…be on her way home from work, and she never answers her cell phone when she's driving."

"Is there somebody else I could call? A friend or relative? I think somebody needs to know that you've been injured. Who's your emergency contact?" He reached for the clipboard with all our emergency sheets.

I had a feeling Bob was my emergency contact. And I sure didn't want Coach Frye to call him.

"You don't have to call anyone," I said quickly. "It really doesn't hurt very much. And the game's almost over. I can just sit here and rest until Angela's mom picks us up."

Coach Frye checked my forehead again and frowned. "Well, just take it easy, okay? I don't like to mess around with head injuries."

I spent the rest of the time sitting on the bench with an ice pack pressed against my forehead. Which, aside from the pain, wasn't a bad way to spend a softball game.

* * *

"What happened to you?" Mom asked the second I walked into the kitchen. She was rinsing grapes in the sink.

"It's that obvious?" I said. Angela and Coral had helped me arrange my bangs after practice. Coral said the bump wasn't really that noticeable. I should've known she was just being nice.

Mom turned off the water and came over to get a better look at me.

"Ow!" I cried when she moved my bangs.

"Did you get hit by a ball?"

"Yes." I eased myself into a chair. "But it's not a big deal." And I didn't want to talk about it. "Mom, there's something else we need talk about. Something important."

"Mmm?" Mom poked at the area around my bump.

I pushed her hand away. "I was going through some boxes in the basement earlier today. And I found one that had a bunch of stuff about Sarah in it. Old photos and newspaper articles and stuff."

Mom froze. She literally froze in place. But then she said, "We should probably get some ice on that bump," and strode across the kitchen as though I hadn't said a word.

"Did you hear what I said?" I asked.

Mom pulled a dish towel out of the drawer, then grabbed a handful of ice cubes from the freezer. "Yes." She wadded the towel around the ice. "I just think we should take care of that bump on your head now."

"I had ice on it for twenty minutes."

"Good." Mom set the towel of ice down in front of me. "Now you can sit for another twenty minutes. You'll thank me for this tomorrow when the swelling's gone down."

I sighed and put the towel to my bump. "There was a lot of stuff in those articles downstairs about how everybody was searching for Sarah," I tried again. "But there wasn't anything in there about her body being found."

"Please, Sam," Mom said, turning her back to me. "It's been a long day. I really don't want to talk about this now."

She went back to rinsing the grapes. The rate she was going, these were going to be the cleanest grapes in town.

"But you'll never want to talk about it," I said. "We never talk about Sarah."

Mom turned off the water again. Was her hand actually shaking?

She leaned against the sink to steady herself for a few seconds, then she slowly turned to look at me. "No, I guess we don't," she said finally. "It's been ten years, but it's still hard for me to talk about her."

I lowered my eyes. "I—I just want to know about those articles in the newspaper," I said. I didn't want to get into a huge thing with Mom. But I had to know. "Why wasn't there one that said her body was found?"

Mom pressed her lips together, then blinked up at the ceiling a few times. A couple of seconds later, she came over and sank down into the chair beside me. "Because Sarah wasn't ever found," she said quietly.

"She wasn't?" I knew it!

"No."

"How come you never told me?"

"I don't know. It wasn't important—"

"Wasn't *important?*" I cried. It was the difference between life and death. If Sarah's body was never found, she could still be alive.

Mom slumped back in her chair and rubbed the back of her neck. "It was all so long ago. And you were awfully young."

"I was three. That's old enough to remember some stuff."

Mom raised an eyebrow. "You remember Sarah?"

"Of course," I answered immediately. Then I said, "Well, sort of." I wished I remembered *more.*

I reached over and grabbed a banana from the middle of the table. I wasn't really hungry, but peeling it gave me something to do with my hands. "Do you ever think she might still be alive?" I asked.

"No," Mom said firmly.

"Why not?" I set the banana down again. "If Sarah's body was never found, isn't there at least a chance she's alive? Maybe she swam to shore and someone found her and took her? Maybe they just raised her as their own child? Or maybe she ended up at the police station and the police thought she was someone else, so they gave her to the wrong people?"

It was possible, wasn't it?

Mom sighed. "I won't lie to you, Sam. I used to hope she was still alive. I even wondered if your *father*"—she said the word like it was a swear word—"had somehow fabricated the whole thing and hidden her away somewhere."

"What?" I cried. "That's terrible!"

"But I know he didn't—"

"How do you know?" I asked. "Maybe Sarah is alive and well and living with him somewhere right now."

Mom shook her head. "That's not possible," she said. "For one thing, your father and I didn't separate right away after Sarah died, so where would she have been all that time?"

"With friends?" I suggested.

"No." Mom reached for my hand and squeezed. "Listen

to me, Sam. Your father was like a big kid. I think that was what I liked about him—at first." For just a second, there was a brief glimmer of a smile in her eyes. But not on her lips. And the look disappeared almost as suddenly as it had appeared. "But he was also irresponsible and sometimes he acted like he didn't have a brain in his head. He didn't know how to take care of a child. That was why Sarah fell in the quarry in the first place. He couldn't take care of a child for five minutes, so how would he manage for ten years?"

My mom was getting all worked up now just thinking about my dad. I could see it in her narrow, angry eyes and her firm jaw. She blamed him for what happened to Sarah. She probably always would. No wonder they got divorced.

"I had a hard time accepting the fact that Sarah was gone myself," Mom went on. "Believe me, I came up with all the scenarios you've just described and more. But Sarah is gone, Sam. She drowned. She's...dead."

Mom let go of my hand and I pulled it away. "How can you be so sure?" I asked.

She just looked at me as though I should know the answer to that question.

"Because it happened at the quarry?" I guessed.

Mom nodded. "That quarry is two miles long. It's hundreds of feet deep in some places. There's heavy construction equipment and who knows what else at the bottom—"

"You mean under the water?" I asked in disbelief.

Mom nodded again.

"How could they do that? How could they just drop tons of stuff into the water?"

"I think it was left there from when they stopped mining the quarry. They filled it with water back in the fifties and that was that."

I played with the fringe on the tablecloth while I thought about the things Mom had just told me. I didn't know what to think.

"Still," I said softly, refusing to give up. "Without a body, isn't it *possible* Sarah survived?"

Mom shook her head sadly. "No, Sam."

My chest tightened. The thought of someone, anyone, drowning in three hundred feet of murky water—her body drifting down, down, down to a graveyard of abandoned construction equipment—made me feel like I was drowning, too.

"It's hard…without a body," Mom said. "That's why we held a funeral and I bought a memorial marker. I needed closure."

Closure? It sounded to me as though Mom just gave up. She decided Sarah was dead and that was it.

"I'm sorry you had to come across all those articles, honey," Mom said. "By yourself. I didn't even realize they were in those boxes down there. But maybe it's good that the subject did come up. You and I are closing the door on this chapter of our lives. Bob and I will be married soon and we'll all be living in a whole new house. It's time to look forward and put the past behind us."

Easy for Mom to say. I had feeling it was a lot easier to put an ex-husband behind you than a father and a sister.

Chapter Six

I had absolutely no motivation for doing anything that night. I didn't even feel like reading. All I did was stare out my bedroom window. I noticed Mrs. Sandvick's two grandsons were out splashing in the little kiddie pool on the patio next door. Their names were Ryan and Josh. Ryan was four, Josh was five. They lived in California and had two turtles and a lizard, and they were here for the whole summer because their parents were backpacking in Europe. I learned all that and more one day when Mrs. Sandvick asked me to baby-sit for them.

I reached into my pocket and pulled out the photo of Sarah and me that I'd found in the basement. I stared at it and thought about how much Sarah and I had missed not growing up together.

As twins, we would've been best friends, I was sure of it. We would've shared a bedroom and stayed up half the night whispering secrets to one another. When we were younger, we probably would've dressed alike, but we would've given that up when we started middle school. We definitely would have had the same taste in clothes, though, so we could've traded clothes once we stopped dressing alike. We probably would have had a lot of the same tastes. But not in boys. We never would've competed for the same boys.

Thinking about Sarah so much was making me depressed. I've always known I had a sister who died, but I never really thought much about it before. Not like this. But ever since I found those articles it seemed like I couldn't stop thinking about Sarah and how things could have been.

I needed to get my mind on something else. I slipped the photo in a book and slid it under my bed. Then I wandered down the hall to see what my mom was doing. From the kitchen window I spotted Bob's silver Saturn parked in our driveway. He came over almost every night now, but he and my mom never really did much. They watched TV or played board games or worked on this 3-D puzzle of Camelot, which was what they were doing now.

Bob's really into 3-D puzzles. He says they relax him. They prove there is order in the universe. You just look at the pieces and match up the pictures. And when you're done you end up with this perfect little miniature of some famous building.

I thought that was a really bizarre way of looking at puzzles, but my mom totally bought it. I bet it was the order-in-the-universe thing that made her fall in love with him. She's into order. So a couple weeks ago Bob brought over the Camelot puzzle and my mom set up a card table in the corner of our living room and they've been building the thing off and on ever since.

I don't think they saw me standing there in the doorway. Every time one of them put two pieces together they'd lean toward each other and kiss.

"These two don't go together," Bob said, pulling two pieces apart.

Mom shrugged. "Do you want your kiss back?"

"I think so." Bob guided my mom out of her chair and into his lap and they started going at it like a couple of high school kids. I could hardly believe it. Who knows what might have happened if I hadn't cleared my throat right then.

They both jumped.

"Sam!" Bob said, all embarrassed.

My mom wiped her mouth on the back of her hand and they pulled away from each other real quick. Like, oh no, we weren't kissing.

"Should I go someplace else?" I asked. Was this what it was going to be like when they were married?

"No!" Mom said sharply.

"Absolutely not," Bob said. He leaped up and pulled out a chair for me. "In fact, why don't you join us?"

Join them? He had to be kidding.

"Yes, you like puzzles, Sam," Mom said, fluffing her hair. "Sit down."

I stared at my mother. *I like puzzles?* When was the last time she saw me put a puzzle together? In fact, when had she *ever* seen me put a puzzle together?

They both shoved piles of puzzle pieces toward me. Bob peered closer at me. "What's that on your forehead?"

I touched my fingers to that bump on my forehead. "Nothing," I said, flipping my bangs over it. "I got hit by a ball at softball practice, that's all."

"You're supposed to catch with your mitt, not your fore-head," Bob said, smiling.

Ha ha. What a funny guy my mom was marrying.

"Hey." Bob elbowed me in the ribs. "That was what my dad said to me when I got hit in the head with a baseball. I didn't find it very amusing, either." Then he told us all about how it was the last game of the season and he was standing in the outfield waiting for the batter to hit one when this beautiful red-tailed hawk sailed by overhead. While Bob was watching the hawk, this kid who'd never gotten a hit all season whacked the ball out to left field, where it promptly hit Bob in the head.

My mom smiled at Bob and patted his arm. I could tell she was enjoying this little family moment. She probably hoped Bob and I would bond over our shared ball injuries. But his story didn't change anything between us. He was still the same old Bob. I was still the same old Sam. And the only thing we had in common was my mom.

The phone rang and I picked up the cordless next to my mom. "Hello?"

"Sam?" It was Angela. She sounded upset. "Can you talk?" she asked in a small voice.

"Yeah, sure," I said, relieved to get away from the happy couple. I took the phone down to my room. "What's wrong?" I kicked the door closed, then flopped on my bed next to Sherlock. He didn't look at all happy about being disturbed.

"I talked to my father this afternoon," Angela said as I reached over to scratch Sherlock under his chin. "Andrew and I are supposed to go visit him next week."

I stopped scratching. A hollow spot opened up in my chest. "Wow, that's great," I said, trying to sound happy for her.

But she didn't sound very happy herself. "Do you know how long it's been since I've seen my father, Sam?"

I thought back. She didn't see him last summer. And I didn't think she saw him the summer before that, either.

"Three years, Sam. Three *years!* What kind of father doesn't see his kids for three years?"

I couldn't answer that. It had been a lot longer than that since I'd seen my dad.

Sherlock butted his head up against my hand, so I started scratching again.

"And it's not like Hill Valley is even that far away," Angela went on.

All I knew about Hill Valley was it was in Minnesota and it was where Angela used to live before her parents got divorced and she moved here in second grade.

"Well, at least you get to see him now," I said. She was so lucky.

"I don't know. What's the point? It's not like he actually wants us to come."

I couldn't understand why she had to be so negative all the time. "He wouldn't have invited you if he didn't want you to come," I pointed out.

"He didn't invite us. My mom called him up and told him he had to see us this summer. She was in her room, but

I heard her. She said he had to let us come sometime before the summer was over or else."

"Or else what?"

"I don't know. All I know is he's supposed to have us a week at Christmas and two weeks during the summer. But for the last three years he's always had some excuse. First he and what's-her-face eloped, then they had some trip, then she got pregnant, then the baby was born, and he's always going to some medical convention or another. But he's used up all his excuses. My mom said pick a week, and he picked next week. Never mind that I have two softball games and Andrew's supposed to work. He picked next week, so we have to go. Whether we want to or not."

It wasn't fair. Angela didn't want to see her dad, but she had to go anyway. I wanted to see my dad more than anything, and I probably never would. I was so jealous I could hardly see straight.

"It won't be as terrible as you think, Angela," I said. "You'll see. You'll get to know each other again. You'll probably have a great time."

"I'll have a miserable time," Angela argued. "But so will our father and what's-her-name, his new wife. We'll all get to be miserable together. Let's talk about something else. How's your forehead? Does it hurt a lot?"

"No, it's okay. But guess what? I talked to my mom about all those articles and stuff we found in the basement this morning." I told Angela what my mom had said about Sarah's body not being found.

"That's bizarre," Angela said.

"Yeah," I said glumly. "But my mom says there's no way Sarah could still be alive."

"Well, of course not," Angela said. "That quarry's pretty deep."

"I know," I said with a heavy sigh.

Angela was right. I knew in my head that there was no way Sarah could still be alive. But somewhere way down deep in my heart was a little voice that wanted to believe there was at least a tiny possibility my sister had somehow survived.

Chapter Seven

Someone was calling me. "S-a-a-am…S-a-a-am…"

It was dark out. Really dark, and cold, too. About the only things I could see were the little white puffs of air I was making every time I breathed out.

"S-a-a-am…"

I shivered. "Sarah? Is that you?"

"Yes. Sa-a-am, come here…" The voice trailed away.

"Where are you?" I didn't know where I was, much less where she was. I knew I was on some dirt path, surrounded by trees. I could hear water in the distance. But I didn't know where we were and I couldn't see anything.

"Please, Sam…"

"I'm trying!" I opened my eyes as wide as they would go and groped around in the darkness, terrified I would run into something. "It's too dark. Where are you?"

"I'm right he-eere…"

Where? I tried to follow her voice, but I couldn't tell where it was coming from.

"Are you by the water?"

"Yes."

"Okay. Hang on, Sarah. I'm coming!" I started running, my bare feet slapping against the hard ground. There were sharp rocks and sticks in my path, but my sister needed me. I had to keep going.

Then my foot caught the bottom of my long nightgown. My hands and knees hit the ground. Hard.

Tears stung my eyes. "Where are you?" I cried, pounding my fists into the dirt.

"I told you, I'm right here! Hurry, Sam! Hurry!"

I clambered to my feet. I didn't know which way to go.

"Where?" I cried desperately. "Where are you?"

"Over here..."

The trees parted and all of a sudden I found myself at the edge of a lake. Finally I saw her: My sister. She was my age and she had on a long white nightgown exactly like mine. Her white-blond hair fanned out around her shoulders. She looked exactly like me.

She was about a hundred feet out, standing—no, floating—just above the water. She reached out her hand for me. "Come with me, Sam."

But I couldn't go with her. I couldn't stand on top of the water like she could. If I tried, I would surely drown. "No, you come over here," I called to her.

"I can't, Sa-a-am. You have to come to me..." She was drifting further away.

"No," I cried. "Don't go! Don't leave me here!"

"Come with me, Sa-a-am...ple-e-ease..." She was almost gone.

"Sarah! Sarah!" I screamed.

"Sam?" I felt a hand on my shoulder.

I turned and a bright light shone in my face. I covered

my eyes with my hands. But my hands were…*wet.* So were my knees.

"Samantha? Are you all right?" someone asked.

I slowly lowered my hands. I was resting on my knees. In a body of water. But it wasn't a lake, it was a pool. A little kid's inflatable backyard pool. And the light in my face was a back porch light.

"Oh my goodness, what are you doing, Sam?" My mom had hold of my arm.

"Is she all right, Suzanne?" Mrs. Sandvick called from her back porch.

By then it was all starting to make sense. I was in the Sandvicks's yard next door. This was their inflatable pool.

How incredibly embarrassing.

I wasn't wearing any long, white nightgown. Instead I had on my usual navy nightshirt that barely covered my butt. I leapt away from both the pool and my mother and tried to pull my nightshirt down a little farther, but it didn't stretch as far as I wanted it to. Luckily at this time of night the only people up were me, my mom, and Mrs. Sandvick. And Mrs. Sandvick's eyes probably weren't real good.

"She's fine, Mrs. Sandvick, thanks." Mom waved at our neighbor. "She just had a bad dream and sleepwalked out here."

A bad dream? It was all just a dream? Sarah wasn't calling me?

Of course she wasn't. She drowned ten years ago.

But it had all seemed so *real.*

"Come on, Sam." Mom put her arm around me and led me back to our house.

"Get some sleep, Suzanne," Mrs. Sandvick called. "You too, Sam."

Mom held the back door for me. "You haven't sleep-walked in years, honey," she said as I stepped into our kitchen.

Huh? "I used to sleepwalk?" I didn't know that.

"Back when you were little," she told me. "It usually happened when you were upset about something. Are you upset about…you know, what we talked about earlier?"

I turned away. "No, no. I'm not upset," I said. I went to the cabinet and reached for a glass.

"Good," Mom said, as I poured myself a glass of water. "Because there's no reason you should be. All that happened a long time ago."

"I know," I said. But if it was so long ago, why did the pain feel so fresh?

* * *

"Angela! Sam!" Coral waved to us.

It was Tuesday afternoon and Angela and I had decided to go to the water park.

Dodging towels and moms and little kids, we made our way around the splash pool and found a spot over by Coral and some other girls we knew from school. They had claimed a group of lounge chairs by the deep pool, in perfect view of Kyle Jenkins, a cute sophomore who was lifeguarding today.

There weren't any chairs left, so Angela and I spread out our towels on the ground next to Tara Huntley and Melissa Holt. We all slathered suntan lotion on each other's backs and combed our hair and talked. Angela told everyone about her upcoming trip to visit her father. Coral complained about her mom. And for the zillionth time, Melissa repeated the story of her big breakup with Dylan Kane. The girl was never going to get over it.

While Melissa was talking I noticed a little girl in the pool. She had on a one-piece swimming suit with a big pink fish on her stomach. And a memory came to me, clear as anything. *Sarah had a swimsuit with a big pink fish on it.* I had one just like it, only my fish was yellow, and I liked hers better—

"Earth to Sam." Coral waved her hand in front of my face.

I blinked. My friends were all staring at me.

"What?" I tucked my hair behind my ear.

Melissa shifted on her towel and rolled her eyes like it was a big deal for her to repeat herself. "I *said,* I heard your mom's getting married."

"Oh. Yeah. Next month." The little girl with the fish suit climbed out of the pool, then cannonballed back in with a big splash.

"Do you get to be in the wedding?" Melissa asked.

"Yup."

"You are *so* lucky!" Melissa squealed.

"And Bob is really nice," Angela put in.

I pulled my knees up to my chest. "Bob is nice." I couldn't argue with that. "But..." They wouldn't understand.

"You wish you knew where your father was," Angela said.

"Yes," I said.

"Why don't you know where your father is?" Coral asked. Her parents were actually still married to each other. In her world, parents didn't get divorced. And dads didn't go years and years without seeing their kids.

"He left when my parents got divorced," I said. "My mom has no idea where he is. And neither does anyone else."

"Well, people don't just disappear," Coral said. "I bet you could find him if you tried."

"She's tried," Angela said in a tired voice. "Believe me, she's tried."

"I've tried everything—the Internet, the library, all of our neighbors."

"She even tried a psychic!" Angela blurted out.

I glared at her. Had it ever occurred to Angela that maybe I didn't want people knowing about that?

"A *psychic?*" Melissa squealed. "Oooh! What was that like?"

I shrugged. "It was okay."

"What about a private detective?" Coral suggested.

"I can't afford a private detective," I said. "And even if I could, where would I find one who'd work for a thirteen-year-old?"

"How about online?" Coral suggested. "I bet you could find someone cheap online. And they'd never have to know you're only thirteen."

Hmm. "I never thought of that."

"Yeah, but you have to be careful," Angela said. "There are a lot of scams online."

"Plus you'd probably need a credit card to pay for it," Melissa put in.

"I have a credit card," I said.

"You have a credit card?" Melissa raised an eyebrow.

"Well, sort of. My mom got me a debit card a few months ago and told me I could use it for an emergency."

"This isn't an emergency," Angela said.

It was as far as I was concerned. Okay, maybe it wasn't the kind of emergency my mom had in mind. But if that card would help me find my dad, I was willing to use it.

I turned to Coral. "How do you find a detective online?"

"We get ads for them all the time in our junk e-mail. Don't you?"

"I don't think so. Could we go over to your house and look at those ads? See if we can find someone to hire?"

Coral squinted at me. "Right now?"

I glanced at my watch. "Sure. We don't have softball for almost two hours."

"You're serious about this?" Angela asked. "Don't you think you're getting a little carried away? How are you going to explain the charge to your mom when she sees her bank statement?"

I shrugged. "I'll worry about that when the time comes."

"Well, count me out," Angela said, getting up and turning over on her towel. "Our moms talk, you know. If my mom finds out about this, I'll probably end up in just as much trouble as you."

I rolled my eyes. "I'm not going to get in trouble!"

"Right," Angela said.

"I'll pass, too," Melissa said, stretching out on her chair. "I need to tan at least twenty minutes on this side or I'll be uneven."

Coral sat up in her chair. "Well, I'm done with the rays. So if you want to come over to my house right now, I don't mind leaving."

Angela shook her head with disapproval. But I didn't see what the big deal was. My mom probably wouldn't even notice the charge. And if she did, well, I'd pay her back.

So Coral and I gathered up our stuff, picked up our pool passes, and biked down the street to her house.

When we got there, her little brother and three of his friends were hunched around the computer in the family room. And her mother was using the computer in the kitchen. But there was a third computer upstairs, in Coral's bedroom. I swear, these people had more computers than people in their family.

"All our computers are networked, so we can still get into my dad's e-mail files from here," Coral said as she booted up her computer.

She grabbed the mouse and opened the e-mail program. She clicked a couple more times and a list of e-mail messages filled the screen.

Coral scanned the list. "Here we go." She clicked on a

line that read "Find anyone, anywhere. Guaranteed!"

"Do you think that's a good one?"

Coral shrugged. "Let's check out his website." She double-clicked on the link and a website came up.

"Whoa. He charges seventy-nine ninety-nine," Coral said.

I just about choked. "That's a little much to put on my mom's debit card."

"I think we can do better than that," Coral said. She pulled up a search engine and typed in "find anyone." There were thousands of matches. But Coral went right down the list, clicking from one website to another so fast she made my head spin.

Finally she stopped. "This one looks pretty good."

"Hey, they even tell you how they find people." I read the list out loud. "'Motor vehicle registration records, voter registration records, national telephone listings, property ownership records, consumer credit reporting agencies, magazine subscription databases, pilot licenses, and more.' This guy sounds good. Can we find out how much he charges?"

Coral scrolled to the bottom of the page. "Nineteen ninety-nine."

"That's not bad," I said, nodding.

"Should we go with him?" Coral asked.

"Sure."

"Okay." Coral read from the form. "First we need your e-mail address."

"But my mom can read all my e-mail." I didn't know

whether she *would* read it, but I didn't want to take any chances. I could just hear her if she suddenly came across an e-mail with my dad's address in it.

"I guess we can use my e-mail address and I can let you know when I hear something," Coral offered. "My mom and dad never check my e-mail."

"Okay." That worked for me.

"Now we need to type in what we know about your dad. The more information we can include, the better."

We filled in his name and we put my address in the blank for "former address."

"What about birthday?" Coral asked.

I shook my head. I didn't even know when my dad's birthday was. "I know he's around thirty-three, though. My mom's thirty-two."

So we counted back and figured out what year my dad had probably been born.

"Every little bit helps," Coral said, typing the information in. "Anything else?"

I squinted at the choices on the screen. I had no idea what city or state my dad lived in, what his Social Security number was, whether he practiced any religion, whether he was affiliated with any groups, or anything else. The only thing left to fill in was my credit card information.

I dug the card out of my wallet and Coral typed it in. Then she scrolled back over everything else we'd already typed in so we could double-check it. "Looks good. Should I click on 'Submit'?" Coral asked.

I bit my lip. There was still time to back out.

But I wasn't going to.

"Click on 'Submit,'" I said.

Now all I had to do was wait.

Chapter Eight

That night I dreamed about Sarah again. This dream wasn't as vivid. In fact, I think I was even aware I was dreaming. But I didn't want the dream to end.

We were here in this house and we were playing hide-and-seek. I'm not sure how old we were. Older than three, but not as old as I am now.

"Come find me, Sam!" she called in a giggly voice.

I searched for her in the front closet, behind the living room couch, under the kitchen table. Finally I found her in my mom's room, crouched behind a chair. She came out laughing. "Again, Sam! Again!"

So we did it again. I pressed my forehead against our front door and counted. "One, two, three…" When I got to twenty, I went to look for her again. It went on like that several times, with her doing all the hiding and me doing all the seeking.

Then I said, "I want to hide this time. You count and I'll hide. Then you can come find me."

Sarah tipped her head back. "Silly! You can't hide. Everybody knows where you are. But nobody knows where I am."

And then I woke up.

Nobody knows where I am.

I opened my eyes and blinked a few times in the darkness. I rolled over and checked my clock. 2:14 A.M. I groaned. It was still nighttime. I hugged my stuffed monkey to my chest and tried to go back to sleep, but I was wide awake.

I turned on my reading lamp, then leaned over the edge of my bed and slid the photo of Sarah and me out from my book.

Nobody knows where I am.

Things always seem kind of creepy at night when you're alone in your room and everything's all dark, but I couldn't help but wonder whether my sister was somehow trying to communicate with me through my dreams. We were twins, after all. We had a connection to one another that other people didn't have.

I stared at the photo, looking for… I'm not sure what I was looking for, but whatever it was clearly wasn't there.

I lay back on my pillow and sighed. I tried to remember what it was like when Sarah was here. What it felt like to have a sister. But no matter how hard I strained my brain, all I could remember were tiny bits and pieces.

A little glass bird that hung in the window and spun around. A humming noise in the bedroom like a fan or a humidifier. Somebody throwing up. Was that me? Or Sarah?

I also remembered high-heeled shoes clicking on the kitchen floor and a dog barking and my mom yelling and a little kid crying…but nothing came together to form a real scene that made sense. The memories were there, though.

Memories of what it was like when we were a family. I could feel them hanging there in the air, inches beyond my fingertips. I just couldn't grab any of them. And the harder I tried, the heavier my eyelids grew.

At some point I must have fallen asleep, because the next time I opened my eyes my bedroom was bright with sunlight. It didn't even feel like I'd slept, but obviously I had. I sat up and rubbed my eyes.

It was nine o'clock now. My mom was at work. Which meant Sherlock and I had the house to ourselves. I got up and went about my morning routine, but I felt off balance somehow, like something was out of place.

Maybe it was that bump on my forehead. I lifted my bangs and peered at myself in the mirror. The purplish bump was still there, but it looked better. The swelling had gone down some.

No, it wasn't the bump that was troubling me. It was this sort of sixth-sense feeling that my sister was still alive. That she was out there somewhere, searching for me. Maybe it was a twin thing. I felt it in the middle of the night when everything was shadowy and unreal. But I also felt it now. In the light of day. It was *real*.

I already knew what my mom would say if I told her that. She'd say "There's no such thing as a sixth sense. Sarah is dead. It's time to move on." But would my dad see it the same way? After all, he was there when the canoe tipped over. His opinion would carry more weight than my mom's. If this detective that Coral found online actually found him, I could talk to him about all this. Who knows? Maybe he'd even help me look for Sarah.

Which made me wonder…had Coral gotten an answer from that guy yet? I decided to call her and find out.

"Hold on, let me check," Coral said groggily when she answered her phone. "I just woke up, so I haven't checked my e-mail yet."

I waited while her computer booted up and she checked her e-mail.

"Doesn't look like it," she said after a little bit. "But we just filled out that form yesterday, you know. It could take a few days to hear back."

"Yeah, I guess. Thanks for checking." We hung up.

A very long day stretched out ahead of me. I had no idea what I was going to do with myself. I figured I could go down in the basement and pack up more boxes, but once I got down there I didn't feel like doing any packing. So I went back to my room.

I hadn't practiced my flute in a couple days. I snapped open my flute case and twisted the three sections together. But I didn't feel like practicing either. Finally I got out my bike.

I don't know whether this was something I decided to do or whether my bike was somehow on autopilot. But I got on it and started pedaling. And before I knew it, I found myself heading down Sixth Street. Sixth Street took me to Rockford Road, which eventually became a gravel road. Old Quarry Road.

I couldn't remember the last time I'd been out this way. Maybe I hadn't ever been out here. I doubt my mom ever went. So who else would have brought me?

It was a really quiet road. There were no houses along

the way. No cars or other people out on bikes. No animals. Not even any wind through the trees. The only sound was my bike tires crunching the gravel.

I had a feeling I shouldn't be out here. At least not by myself. There wasn't a single person in the whole world who knew where I was. What if I got kidnapped? Or murdered? What if my murderer dumped my body in the quarry and nobody ever found it?

I swallowed hard. My imagination was going crazy. This was Clearwater, Iowa. We didn't have murderers here. But wasn't that what people always said whenever there was a murder in their small town?

The gravel road ended at a small parking area, but there were no cars in the lot. I could sort of see the quarry through the trees. I could smell it, too. It smelled like rotting weeds.

I got off my bike and wheeled it up the narrow dirt path. A mosquito buzzed by my ear. I swatted it away.

I kept going until the trees ended and I came to a chainlink fence. I could see the trees on the other side of the quarry, but I couldn't see down into the pit.

I had to get closer. So I leaned my bike against a tree, then tiptoed up to the fence. It wasn't very high. I stuck my toe in one of the gaps and curled my fingers around the bar along the top of the fence. Then I heaved myself up onto the top of the fence and jumped down to the other side, landing on my hands and knees. I quickly picked myself up and dusted myself off.

This was it. There were just a few feet of tall grass and rock, then the ground just sort of dropped off and the quarry lay down below. A huge mouth of water, ready to swallow me up if I stepped over the edge.

I took a couple of steps back and grabbed for the fence. Then I gazed down at the water again. It was a long way down. Too far to launch a canoe from. So where had my dad put his canoe in?

It was several miles around the whole quarry. He could've done it anywhere. Anywhere but here.

I started walking beside the fence. Every now and then I stopped to scratch my ankles. I hoped it was just the tall grass that was making me itch and not bugs. As I walked, the patch of grass grew wider. And wider. Holding on to the fence for support, I slowly made my way down a steep hill. When I reached the bottom, I found myself standing in a small clearing.

It wasn't so far down to the water here. Maybe a foot or two. I had no idea how deep the water was. People say the quarry is 300 feet deep, but not here at the edge. You probably could get a canoe in here.

I looked around for a long branch. Something I could put in the water and get an idea of how deep it was. I spotted one over by a sign that read "Danger! Absolutely No Swimming, Boating, or Canoeing." I ran over and picked up the branch.

It was about two inches around and stood as tall as my chest. I took it over to the edge of the water and slowly lowered it down. Down, down, down until only the tip where I held it remained out of the water. The other end still hadn't touched bottom. I let the branch go and it bobbed to the surface, then floated out of reach.

I shivered. The water was really murky, just like my mom said. It was so thick and cloudy it didn't wave or ripple or anything. It just sat there, unmoving. Dead.

I could see why Sarah's body was never found. Even with all the fancy equipment the police must use to search for people in the water, it would be impossible to find someone here. And even if the divers had an idea where the person was, they'd have to be careful about going down too deep because they might not see the construction equipment at the bottom and they could ram right into it.

But despite all that, standing here right now, gazing out over the water, that sixth sense was just as strong as it had been back at my house. Maybe even stronger.

I knew Sarah wasn't down there.

* * *

"Are you out of your mind?" Angela asked when I called her later that afternoon.

I couldn't just keep carrying all this around in my head. I had to talk to someone. Obviously I couldn't talk to my mom. I'd never been able to talk to my Grandma Sperling. We didn't see each other enough to have that kind of relationship. If things were different, I might have been able to talk to Bob's mother. If I'd been born into her family, I mean. But the only reason she and I were anything at all to each other was because my mom was marrying her son. Really, the only person I could talk to was Angela.

"I'll say it one more time. There is no way your sister

could still be alive, Sam," Angela said. "You do know that, don't you?"

I didn't answer.

"Your sister is dead, Sam," Angela went on. "She's been dead for ten years." She sounded just like my mother.

"Gee, tell me what you really think," I muttered.

"Do you want me to?" Angela asked seriously.

I shrugged. It didn't matter. Angela always told me what she really thought.

"Well, I think you don't want your mom and Bob to get married."

My mouth dropped open. "That's not true!" I didn't want Bob to adopt me, but I didn't care whether they got married or not.

"I think it is," Angela said. "But you can't tell your mom that, so you're putting all this energy into other stuff. Like looking for your dad. And wondering whether your sister could still be alive. It's, like, some kind of distraction. Because you can't deal with the truth."

No! Angela was wrong. Way wrong.

"If you really want to know what I think, you should quit digging around in the past and concentrate on the future. Bob's a great guy. Why don't you just give him a chance?"

"Yeah, well maybe you should give your real dad a chance, too," I grumbled.

Angela clammed up when I said that. In all the years we'd been friends, I don't think we'd ever had a real fight. But I could tell we were on the verge of one right now.

"You don't know anything about my father, Sam," Angela said coolly.

"No. And you don't know anything about mine. And you don't know anything about my sister, either."

At first Angela didn't say anything. Then in a small voice she said, "Okay, maybe neither one of us should tell the other what to do."

"Maybe not," I agreed, relieved that a fight had been averted.

But nothing had really been solved.

Chapter Nine

After dinner I noticed the little voice mail icon flashing on my cell phone. I immediately dialed in to get my message. "Hey, Sam. It's me, Coral. Call me ASAP."

I had a pretty good idea what that meant.

My mom and Bob were over checking on the progress of our new house, so I didn't have to worry about them walking in on me. I punched in Coral's number. "Hey, it's me," I said anxiously as soon as she picked up the phone. "What's up?"

"I thought you'd like to know we heard back from that detective guy," Coral said.

"We did?" I knew it! I elbowed my bedroom door closed just in case my mom and Bob came home early, then crawled up onto my bed.

"Don't get too excited. I don't have a single, definite address and phone number for you," Coral said. "What I have is three addresses and phone numbers. The e-mail says they're pretty sure one of these Joseph Wrights is the one you're searching for. But if it turns out none of them is, they'll keep looking for free."

"Okay," I said, pulling my legs up under me. My whole body trembled. "So what have you got?" For the first time in ten years, I was about to get some *real* information!

"Do you have something to write with?" Coral asked.

"Yeah." I reached over and grabbed a pencil from my desk and a piece of scratch paper from my garbage can. My hand was shaking so hard I could barely write. But somehow I managed to copy the names, addresses, and phone numbers as Coral read them off. There was one Joseph Wright in San Diego, California, another in Richland, Minnesota, and a third in Omaha, Nebraska.

"Thanks, Coral," I said. "Thanks for everything."

"No problem. Good luck, Sam. I hope you find what you're looking for."

So did I.

At first I just sat cross-legged on my bed, my cell phone in my hand, staring at those names, addresses, and phone numbers. *One of these men was probably my dad.*

Was it possible for a thirteen-year-old to have a heart attack? All I had to do was pick the right number and I could be talking to my dad in about twenty seconds. And even if I didn't pick the right number, there were only two others to try. Five minutes, tops, and I'd know which of those Joseph Wrights was my dad. Assuming one of them was.

With my mom out of the house, this was the perfect time to try and find out. But I'd never been so nervous in my entire life. How was I supposed to make a phone call when I literally could not breathe?

Of course, I didn't have to call these people. I had their addresses, too. I could just write them each a letter. There were two reasons writing might be better. One, I wouldn't have to explain the charge on the phone bill later (though I still might have to explain the charge for hiring the detective). And two, I could take my time and figure out exactly what I wanted to say. But I might have to wait to hear back. And what if the real Joseph Wright never replied? No, calling was definitely the better choice. That way I'd get answers right away. And I'd get to hear my dad's voice.

I just needed to work up the nerve to do it.

I wished I had more than just names, addresses, and phone numbers. I wished I had photographs. And basic information like whether these guys were married or had children. I'd never thought about my dad having a whole new family before. But it was possible.

"Just do it!" I said out loud. "Just pick up the phone and call."

But what was I supposed to say? I argued with myself. "Hi, this is Sam, your long-lost daughter?" What if all he had to say back was "Yeah, so?"

I remembered what Angela said about how when you don't know your dad, you can pretend he's anyone you want him to be. Maybe she was right. Maybe deep down I did just want to pretend. Maybe I didn't want to find out who he really was.

No, I wanted to know who he was. I wanted to know whether he ever thought about me. Whether he ever thought about Sarah.

So…which Joseph Wright should I try first?

Probably the one in San Diego. I knew my dad had been in San Diego seven years ago when he sent me that post-card, so San Diego was a good place to start.

I crept out into the hallway and listened for my mom and Bob. It didn't sound like they were back yet. But if I didn't hurry this up, they would be. I tiptoed back to my room, closed the door, and hopped back up onto my bed. Then I took a deep breath, picked up the phone, and quickly punched in the San Diego number before I could change my mind. The phone felt slippery in my hands. I could feel my heart in my throat. I almost hung up, but I forced myself to hang on until someone finally picked up on the fifth ring.

"Hello?" It was a woman. A woman around my mom's age, it sounded like. My dad's new wife?

"Um, hi," I said. My mind suddenly went blank. Why didn't I at least write out a speech ahead of time?

"Yes?" the woman said.

I swallowed hard, then plunged ahead. "Um, you don't know me. My name is Sam. Sam *Wright.*"

"Yes?" The woman sounded a little impatient now.

My heart was pounding so hard I thought my chest would crack open. "D-d-does that name mean anything to you?" I asked.

"Well, other than the fact we share the same last name, no." The woman sounded nicer this time. "Should it?"

"I don't know," I said. Gee, if this woman was my dad's new wife, this call could come as a huge shock.

"I-I-I'm looking for my father," I stammered. "His name is Joseph Wright. I know there's a Joseph Wright at this number. C-could I maybe talk to him, please?"

"I'm afraid not," the woman replied matter-of-factly. "Joseph died three years ago."

"What?" No!

"But Joseph couldn't have been your father," the woman went on.

I breathed a sigh of relief when she said that. This was the wrong Joseph Wright. My dad was still alive.

But the feeling disappeared almost as suddenly as it had appeared. "Are you sure?" I asked. Wasn't it possible my dad ran off to California after Sarah died, got married, and never told his new wife about me?

"Joseph and I were married for fifteen years. We both wanted children very much, but Joseph..." she broke off.

"What?"

"He couldn't have children," she said softly.

"Oh." I suddenly felt very sorry. And very embarrassed. That was such personal information. And it was none of my business.

I felt bad for this woman. She seemed so nice. I bet her husband, Joseph, was nice, too. He probably would've been a good dad if he had had children.

"Well, thanks anyway," I said, not knowing what else to say. "And—I'm really sorry about your husband." Then I hung up.

Whew! One down, two to go. After making one call, it wasn't quite as hard to do it again. I wiped my slippery hands on my shorts, then punched in the number for the next Joseph on my list. The one in Minnesota.

This time an answering machine picked up.

Goosebumps dotted my arms.

I knew that voice!

I couldn't believe that after all those years, I recognized my dad's voice. But I did. "Yo—" *Yo, Sammy! Yo, Sarah! Yo, Suzanne!* He always said that instead of hello. "We can't come to the phone right now, so leave a message. We'll get back to ya." *Beep!*

I slammed the receiver down.

I could feel the blood pounding inside my head. My hands were shaking. *It was him.* I knew it was him.

I took a deep breath and tried to calm down.

Another breath.

And another.

What was I going to do now?

I got up from my bed and wandered around my room. He was married. Or at least living with someone. The voice on the answering machine had said, *"We'll get back to you."*

I grabbed my pillow, then set it back down. I looked out the window, but my eyes didn't focus. I replayed that voice, *his* voice, over and over inside my head. *Yo. We can't come to the phone right now, so leave a message. We'll get back to ya.*

He was in Minnesota. Just one state away. Just like Angela's dad. Had he been there all this time? Why hadn't he at least called me once in the last however many years? *Why?*

I had to call him back. I had to call him back right now and leave him a message. I picked up the phone and started dialing before I could chicken out.

This time the answering machine picked up on the second ring.

"Yo. We can't come to the phone right now, so leave a message. We'll get back to ya."

"Hello? Dad?...It's me, Sam..." My throat tightened as my eyes filled with tears. "Do you remember me? Please call me," I said. I barely managed to get my cell phone number out before the tears started to roll down my cheeks.

Chapter Ten

I didn't set my cell phone down the rest of the night. *Come on, Dad. Hurry up and call me back before Mom gets home!*

Unfortunately my cell phone stayed silent.

Our other phone, on the other hand, never stopped ringing. First the telephone company called wanting to know if we wanted to switch long-distance providers. Then my mom called to tell me she and Bob were going to a movie, did I want to come (no). Then the stationery store called to say the wedding invitations were in. And then Angela called. She probably called our house line because I didn't answer my cell phone when I saw it was her. I didn't want to tie up that line.

"Angela!" I said when I picked up the phone. "You're never going to believe what happened." I proceeded to tell her all about my evening.

But Angela just couldn't get excited for me. "How do you know that guy is really your dad?" she asked.

"I know it is. I recognized his voice."

"You recognized his voice?" She sounded doubtful. "Sam, it's only been five months since I talked to my father and I hardly recognized his voice."

"You're kidding!" Even for Angela, that sounded extreme.

"Why would I recognize a voice I hardly ever hear?"

"Because he's your dad."

"Father," Angela corrected.

"Whatever." I didn't want to argue over words. "The point is there's a connection between you. A father-daughter connection. You'll always recognize your dad's voice because of that connection."

"I don't know. I don't think so," Angela said. "Look, Sam. I don't know whether this guy is your dad or not. But just because you're father and daughter doesn't mean you're always connected. Sometimes connections get broken."

True. But that didn't mean they had to stay broken.

It was almost ten o'clock when Angela and I hung up. I knew my mom would be home soon. I would've thought that wherever my dad was, he would be getting home soon, too. I could picture him walking into his house. I didn't know what he might look like now. I'd only seen that one picture of him, and it was really old. I imagined a man with really blond hair like mine pressing the message button on his answering machine. I could see the look of surprise on his face when he heard my voice, because of course he'd recognize my voice, too. I could see him replaying that message over and over again just to hear my voice. And I could see him checking a clock on the wall, wondering whether it was too late to call me back.

It's not. I tried to send thought waves through the phone line. *Call me. Please call me.*

He never called that night.

Or the next day.

Or the day after that.

And there were a million reasons why he wouldn't have called. Reasons other than he just didn't want to talk to me. One, he could have been on vacation. Two, he could have been working a lot. Three, maybe he worked nights and slept during the day. That would make it awfully hard to find a good time to call me back.

Right?

It was also possible he had a new wife who had gotten the message and erased it before he'd even heard it. Even if he was perfectly happy to hear from me, a new wife might not be so happy about it. Now that I really thought about it, I probably shouldn't have left a message like that.

Or maybe there was another reason. Maybe he was afraid my mom would answer the phone.

After three days, I figured it was okay to try him again. But what if he really didn't want to talk to me? What if he didn't care about me at all? I couldn't deal with that possibility, so I decided to hold off a couple more days. We were coming up on the weekend. Surely he'd call during the weekend.

But on Saturday Mom had a huge list of things she wanted to do. First she wanted to pick up the wedding invitations. Then she wanted to stop in at the bakery, the florist, and Xavier's, the place where she and Bob were having the wedding reception, just to make sure everything was set. She also had an appointment at Julianne's for her final dress fitting and then she was hoping to meet with the minister to make her final music selections. She and Bob's mother had the whole day planned out, and they wanted to drag me along for all of it.

I hesitated. "I don't know." I was sure my dad was going to call that day and I didn't want to miss him. Sure, I could bring my cell phone along, but I couldn't exactly talk to him in front of my mom.

"Sam, taking care of these last-minute wedding details is supposed to be fun. I would've thought you'd want to come along." Mom sounded hurt.

"Fine," I said with a heavy sigh. "I'll go." It wasn't like I had a choice anyway. So when my mom wasn't looking, I set my phone to vibrate and shoved it in my shorts pocket. At least I'd know whether my dad called or not. Then she and I headed out.

We stopped to pick up Bob's mother first. "Oh, I'm so glad you girls invited me along!" she said as she hopped into the front seat. "We're going to have such a nice day."

Yeah, real nice.

Then the two of them started talking about how close the wedding was and how it was finally going to happen. I just sat in the back with my hand resting on my cell phone and watched the world go by.

We stopped at the florist first. Everything was in order there. Then we stopped at the bakery. Everything was in order there, too. On the way to the stationery store, my mom said, "They were supposed to tile the bathrooms at the new house yesterday. It's not that far out of the way.

Would anyone like to go over and see it?" She glanced pointedly at me in the rearview mirror.

"Oh, I would love to see your new place," Bob's mother said. "I've been by it, you know. But I've never been inside."

"You haven't seen the inside?" Mom asked, sounding surprised.

"No."

"Well, then we're definitely going to stop." Mom put on her turn signal and moved into the left lane. Then she turned onto Ridge Drive. "It's been a while since you've seen the house, too, Sam. It's almost done."

"Great," I said, trying to sound enthusiastic.

"This is such a nice neighborhood," Bob's mom prattled on as we drove past rows of identical two-story beige houses. "Dan and Becky really like it." I couldn't remember whether Dan was Bob's brother or Becky was his sister. Either way, they lived about two blocks from where we were going to live, which my mom considered a huge plus.

"I'm sure we'll be very happy here," Mom said. "Don't you think so, Sam?"

I gave the correct answer, which was "Yes, of course." After all, my mom and Bob were plunking down a huge amount of money for this house. And most of my friends lived nearby. As far as my mom was concerned, there was absolutely no reason I shouldn't be happy here. So, of course, I would be.

Mom pulled up in front of a house that looked just like all the other two-story beige houses on the block. I don't know how she knew which one was ours. There was no grass and no driveway yet. But there were doors on the house now. A front door and probably a garage door, too. Though it was hard to tell for sure because the garage door was up and there was somebody sawing something in the garage.

We all got out of the car and the guy in the garage stopped whatever he was doing. It turned out he was the builder, so he was thrilled to show us around.

Bob's mother had nice things to say about everything— the new cabinets and hardwood floor in the kitchen, the screen porch that wasn't screened in yet, the fireplace in the living room, the ceramic tile in the entryway…. The carpet wasn't in yet in the living room and dining room, but the builder said it was coming in the next couple of days.

He led us up the uncarpeted stairway so we could check out the bedrooms and the freshly tiled bathrooms. My bedroom was the first one at the top of the stairs. There was a guy working on the window seat in there. He had sawdust in his hair, on his face, and all over his shirt. He looked up when he saw me lingering in the doorway.

My mom and Bob's mom had continued on down the hall with the builder.

"Are you the lucky lady who gets this room?" Sawdust Man asked with a wide grin that showed the gap between his two top front teeth.

"Yup." That was me. The lucky lady.

It was a nice room. I loved the built-in bookshelves. And I couldn't complain about the view of the woods from the window. But nice as it was, it just didn't feel like my room.

And the rest of the house didn't feel like my house. It didn't feel like anybody's house. It had no personality. No feelings. No memories.

The thing about houses is they're filled with the memories of all the people who have ever lived in them. Our little house on Hartman Lane has memories of me, my mom, my dad, Sarah, and lots of people I've never even met. Those memories are all part of that house. When we move, my mom and I will remember things that happened when we lived there. But in a way, memories stay with a house. Like ghosts.

I knew exactly what my mom would say to that. She'd say, "Well, I guess we'll just have to create memories for our new house as soon as we can. And there are no such things as ghosts."

The only problem is, this is a huge house. It would take a long time to create enough memories to fill the whole thing. Honestly, I just didn't think I was up to it.

* * *

It had been five days since I'd left the message on my dad's answering machine and he still hadn't called me back. *What is the deal?* I wondered as I paced anxiously back and forth in my room.

Was his answering machine broken? Maybe he got the message, wrote my number down so he could call me back later, but then lost the number? Maybe he'd been tearing his whole house apart like a crazy person, trying to find my number, scared to death he'll never hear from me again.

Or maybe I was wrong? Maybe the person I called wasn't my dad after all?

No. One thing I was sure of—that was my dad's voice on the answering machine.

It couldn't be that he just didn't want to talk to me. That he just didn't care. I remember stuff he used to do, like monkey back rides and monkey faces. He was the monkey man and I was his Sammy Bear. He had to call me back. He just *had* to.

Maybe he was in the hospital? Or maybe he'd been in a terrible accident? What if after all these years I finally found my dad, only to have him die some terrible death before I could make contact with him? Like the Joseph Wright in San Diego did?

Maybe I should call that number again and leave another message? This was a good time to do it—Mom and Bob were busy addressing wedding invitations. They weren't likely to check on me for a while.

I could say something like, "Hey, even if you don't ever want to see me or talk to me again, at least call me back and tell me. Just so I know."

I reached under my mattress and pulled out the scrap of paper with the information about the three Joseph Wrights. I didn't really need the paper, though. I had his phone number memorized.

My heart pounding, I picked up my phone and punched in the number. But this time the phone didn't ring at all. Instead I got a bunch of tones and a recording that said, "We're sorry. The number you have dialed has been disconnected."

Do You Know the Monkey Man?

Disconnected? I stared at the cell phone in my hand. That couldn't be right. I'd just dialed that number five days ago. Maybe my finger slipped and I dialed the wrong number?

I tried again. But all I got was the same recording.

Chapter Eleven

It wasn't fair. I'd tried so hard to find him. And just when I'd gotten close, he slipped away.

Well, I knew where my dad was five days ago. Maybe I could call Information and find out where he went? Maybe there was a forwarding number? I dialed 411.

The operator who answered told me she had listings for two Joseph Wrights and one D. Wright in Richland, Minnesota. I knew I needed the Joseph Wright who lived at 7430 Sheridan Avenue South in Richland, Minnesota. But the lady just said that that number was disconnected and there was no further information.

Argh! "Thanks anyway," I said, hanging up.

I didn't know what else to do, so I called Angela to see if she had any advice.

"Drop it," she said right away. "That's my advice."

"I can't!" I flopped back onto my bed.

"Well, if this guy really is your dad, obviously he's trying to tell you that he doesn't want to talk to you. I'm sorry, Sam, but some fathers are like that. They walk out and then they pretend that whole part of their lives when they were married to your mom never happened. Even if they had kids. They just cut the kids out of their lives, too. Like they don't even care."

Maybe Angela's father was like that, but I never thought mine could be like that, too. I picked at a loose thread on my comforter. "He sent me a postcard when I was six. He cared about me then. What changed since then?"

Angela's voice softened. "See, this is what I was trying to tell you a couple of weeks ago. Back then you could still pretend your dad was a good guy and he loved you and you could tell yourself there were all these good reasons why he hasn't been in your life—" I could tell by the tone of Angela's voice that she was trying to be nice, but her words cut me to the core.

"But now you have to face the truth about him," Angela went on. "And you don't even know the truth. The truth could actually be worse than you're imagining. Your father could be some sort of criminal or something. He could be a drug dealer or a kidnapper or—"

A kidnapper?

"Oh no!" I cried as a new idea took shape in my head. I sat up on my bed.

"I know. It's terrible to think of your own father that way, but—"

"No! Listen to me, Angela," I interrupted. "What if he *is* a kidnapper? What if he...kidnapped my sister?"

Angela let out a short laugh, then cut it off when she realized I was serious.

"That would explain it," I said. "It would explain

everything: why I have this feeling she's still alive, why he hasn't been in touch all these years, why his phone was suddenly disconnected—"

Whoa! What was I saying? That my dad...what? Faked Sarah's death, then took her away? Was that what I really thought? That my dad was the kind of person who would do such a thing?

It was possible. If he really wanted to hurt my mom. Grandma Sperling said my mom and dad never had a good marriage.

Plus Sarah's body was never found. I haven't heard from my dad since I was six years old, and even then I didn't actually see him. I only got a postcard. If my dad had my sister with him (the sister everyone thinks is dead), and then I called him up out of the blue, no way would he call me back. He wouldn't want me to know about Sarah.

"Sam, your father did not kidnap your sister. She drowned in the old quarry ten years ago."

"No, she didn't," I argued. I was nearly one hundred per cent sure of that.

"Sam!"

I could tell Angela thought I'd totally lost my mind, but I didn't care. I needed a plan. I needed to figure out what I was going to do next.

"Angela, do you know where Richland, Minnesota, is?"

"I think it's one of the suburbs near Minneapolis. Why?"

"And how far is Minneapolis from where you're going?"

"I don't know," Angela said warily. "An hour to an hour and a half—"

Angela was going to Minnesota *tomorrow.* "I've got to go to Minnesota with you," I said. "Can I?" If I could get as far as Hill Valley with Angela, maybe once I was there I could figure out how to get the rest of the way to Richland.

"What?" Angela cried.

I took a deep breath. "I need to go to 7430 Sheridan Avenue South in Richland and meet Joseph Wright and find out why his phone is disconnected."

But I knew if I was right about all this, if this Joseph Wright was my dad, and if he really did fake my sister's death and kidnap her all those years ago, he probably didn't just disconnect his phone. He probably took Sarah and ran.

"Sam, you're scaring me," Angela said. "This is just too crazy...."

Still, I could go to 7430 Sheridan Avenue South and find out whether anyone was living there. Even if no one was, I could go to the neighbors and find out whether the man who had lived there had a young girl with him. Maybe I could even get a clue to where they went.

"Please, Angela," I begged. "I need to go to Minnesota with you!"

"I don't know, Sam," Angela said. "If you really think this is what happened, I think you need to tell your mom—"

"She won't believe me!" She was too wrapped up in wedding plans to even listen to me. *You and I are closing the door on this chapter of our lives. It's time to look forward and put the past behind us.*

"Well, then maybe you could talk to Bob?" Angela suggested. "He's a cop. Maybe he could—"

"I'm definitely not talking to Bob! Not about this. Come on, Angela. Please?" I pleaded. "If I can get to Hill Valley, I can maybe take a bus to Richland. Then I can go over to that house and see what I can find out. It is possible I'm wrong about all this, you know—" I didn't think so, but I knew Angela was more likely to give in if I said it.

"If I'm wrong, I'll just come back to Clearwater with you and pretend it never happened," I promised. "But if I'm right, don't you think I have a right to know?"

Angela didn't say anything right away. Was she starting to come around?

"I'd be with you in Hill Valley most of the time," I went on. "We'd have fun. You could show me around and we could...well, I don't know what there is to do in Hill Valley."

"Not much," Angela grumbled. "But now that you mention it, it might be nice to have you there at my father's. Especially if things don't go well."

Yes!

"I'll call him and see whether he'll let me bring a friend, okay?"

"Okay!" I squealed. "Thanks, Angela. Thank you so much."

I was practically bouncing off the walls waiting for her to call me back. Oh my gosh! What if Sarah really was alive and living with my dad? The thought gave me goosebumps.

Except...my mom and dad didn't get divorced right away when Sarah died. So how could my dad have kidnapped her? Where would he have hidden her all that time? And if he really was a kidnapper, why did he just take *her?* Why wouldn't he have taken me, too?

Okay, maybe it didn't all fit together as well as I wanted it to. But there was one thing I did know. The voice on the answering machine was definitely my dad's. That was why I had to go to Richland, Minnesota.

Come on, Mr. Hunter. Please say yes!

Of course, I still needed to clear it with my mom. So I did what I could to pull myself together. I took several deep breaths and ran my fingers through my hair. Then I calmly went to see how she and Bob were coming on the wedding invitations.

I was surprised to find her alone. But there she was, reading a magazine on the couch in the family room, Sherlock sound asleep in her lap. Except for the stack of stamped wedding invitations piled on the coffee table, it was just like how things were a year ago. Before she and Bob got engaged and started spending every waking minute together.

"Where's Bob?" I asked.

She looked up and smiled. "He's got an early meeting in the morning, so he had to get home."

"Oh." I perched on the edge of the couch. "Angela's going to visit her dad tomorrow."

"Yes, I know." Mom set her magazine aside. "I talked to Anne today. I understand Angela's not very happy about this trip."

"No, she's not," I agreed. "She doesn't like her dad very much." I picked up *TV Guide* and paged through it.

"Actually, she invited me to go with her," I said casually.

"It's okay, isn't it? She really needs some moral support."

"Moral support?" Mom cocked her head at me as though wondering what I was trying to get away with now.

"Yeah." I turned the page in *TV Guide* like it was no big deal. But inside my heart was hammering. It was the biggest deal in the world!

"It's only six days. I'll be back next Sunday night." If I acted like it wasn't a big deal, maybe she would, too.

"You can't go, Sam," Mom said quietly but firmly.

"What?" I sat up. "Why not?"

Mom looked surprised that I would even ask. "My bridal shower is on Saturday."

Crud! I'd forgotten all about that.

"This is important, Mom," I said in as reasonable a voice I could muster. "I really have to go with Angela. She'll be totally miserable if I don't."

Sherlock raised his head and glanced from one of us to the other, then hopped down and scampered away.

Mom shifted her position so her whole body was facing me. "Bob's mother and all his sisters and sisters-in-law have been planning this shower for months," she explained. "They've worked very hard. How would it look if my own daughter didn't show up?"

"Who cares how it looks!" I shouted, leaping to my feet. I slammed *TV Guide* down on the coffee table and accidentally knocked a few of the wedding invitations to the floor. "You're always so concerned about what Bob's family thinks!"

Her face tight, Mom leaned over to pick up the invitations. She didn't even respond to what I said. All she said was, "I'm sorry, Sam. But the answer is no."

I felt a pain in my chest. I was too old for a temper tantrum, but tears stung my eyes. How could she say no?

"It's not fair!" I said, even though I knew that argument never worked with her.

She shot me a warning look.

"It's *your* shower, not mine. And it's just one day. I can't believe you'd say no because of one day. Angela *needs* me, Mom!" I pleaded.

But Mom wasn't buying it. "I need you, too," she said in a small voice.

"No, you don't," I muttered. "All you need is Bob and his mother and the rest of his stupid family." With that, I stormed up to my bedroom.

I half expected her to follow me and tell me I was wrong, but she didn't. And the fact that she didn't made me even madder.

I was really fuming when the phone rang a few minutes later. It was Angela. "I talked to my father," she said. "I didn't say anything about you wanting to go to Richland or anything. I just asked if I could bring a friend." She paused. "He said yes."

"H-he did?"

"Yeah. Did you ask your mom? Did she say it was okay, too?"

"I talked to her." Then words popped out of my mouth before I could stop them. "She said it's okay. You guys can pick me up whenever you're ready tomorrow."

Chapter Twelve

I'd never done anything like this before. Sure, I'd told a few little white lies now and then. Hasn't everyone? But I'd never gone ahead and done something my mom specifically said I couldn't do. Of course, she'd never said I couldn't do something so important before, either. My entire life hinged on this trip to Minnesota.

I had set my alarm for 7:00 A.M., the time my mom usually left for work, but I was wide awake at 6:30. I had wondered whether I'd see things differently after a good night's sleep, whether I'd change my mind about going. But I was just as determined to go today as I'd been last night.

For half an hour I lay in bed scratching Sherlock's chin and listening to my mom move around the house getting ready for work. I felt a little bit guilty, knowing what I was about to do (Boy, was she going to mad when she got home and found me gone!), but not guilty enough to change my mind. Eventually she'd understand why I had to do this. Maybe she'd even thank me one day. If I actually found Sarah as well as my dad.

Do You Know the Monkey Man?

At 6:45 I heard my bedroom door open. I squeezed my eyes closed and pretended I was asleep until I heard my door latch shut again. I don't think I even breathed until I heard the garage door going up and the car starting.

As soon as I heard the garage door coming back down, I rolled over and switched my alarm off. Then I threw off my covers and leaped to my window. I stuck my finger between two slats of mini blinds and watched my mom back down the driveway. By the time she got home this afternoon, I'd already be in Minnesota.

I let the blinds drop back into place and raced to my closet. I hadn't dared to pack anything last night, just in case my mom walked in. But now I hauled my suitcase down from the shelf in my closet and filled it with clothes, makeup, a hair dryer, and a curling iron. I put on a pair of shorts and a T-shirt, then quickly ran a comb through my hair. I pulled out the photo of me and Sarah and stuck it in my purse. Finally I grabbed the book I was reading so I'd have something to do on the long car ride.

Last I went to the kitchen to write Mom a note.

Dear Mom,

I'm sorry, but I had to do this. I had to go with Angela. I know you'll be mad, but I had to do it anyway. I'll explain why when I get back.

Love, Sam

P.S. I hope your shower is nice.

I grabbed my cell phone and popped it into my purse. As I did, I realized that probably the first thing Mom would do when she read my note was call my cell phone and ream me out. So I picked up my cell phone, hit the power button, then dropped it back into my purse.

Would she call Angela's dad's house then? I doubted she knew the number, but she could probably get it easily enough from Angela's mom. Well, there wasn't much I could do about that. Fortunately it was too far of a trip for her to just drive up there and drag me home by my ear. I knew that if I managed to get there, she'd have to let me stay the whole week. And then, one way or another, I'd find a way to get myself to Richland.

I double-checked my suitcase to make sure I had everything. Then I went to the front door to wait for Angela and her brother.

At exactly seven minutes past eight they pulled into the driveway. I have to say, Andrew Hunter did not drive a very cool car. It was old and brown and extremely rusty, but it ran. And it was all his.

I hadn't seen much of Andrew lately, but let me tell you, he was looking mighty fine when he stepped out of that rust bucket of a car. He'd been working in the lumberyard at Menards all summer, and lifting all those heavy planks of wood had done beautiful things to his arms. I really regretted not taking a little more time with my hair that morning.

"Hey, Sam," he said as he popped the trunk. My knees turned to jelly when he grabbed my suitcase and tossed it in the trunk with the others, but somehow I managed to get myself into the backseat with Angela.

"I'm glad you talked me into this," Angela said, moving her purse over to make room for me. "It'll be a lot easier to handle my dad if you're there, too."

I squeezed her hand. I was glad she was happy to have me along. "Everything will be fine," I told her. "You'll see."

"Ready to roll, ladies?" Andrew eyed us through the rearview mirror. I loved how he called us "ladies."

I buckled my seat belt. "Ready," I said.

As Andrew backed down the driveway, I leaned over and whispered to Angela, "I can't believe your mom's letting him drive all the way to Minnesota!" He'd just turned sixteen four months ago, so he hadn't been driving all that long.

In fact, if my mom had originally said I could go, but then found out Andrew was driving, she probably would've changed her mind.

Angela shrugged. "My mom didn't want to drive us. She doesn't want to see my dad or his new wife. And Andrew really wanted a car up there. That's about all he cares about these days. He didn't care whether we went or not, as long as he got to have his car. So letting him drive seemed like a good solution all around. Besides, it's mostly interstate between here and Hill Valley and there isn't a lot of traffic."

"Hey, Angela," Andrew said, not taking his eyes off the road. "You've got the map back there, don't you?"

Angela pulled a map out of the pocket in the back of

Andrew's seat. "Right here." She held it up. A yellow high-lighter line marked our route on the map.

"Good. I think I know where we're going, but I might need you to look at the map along the way."

"Whatever," Angela replied.

As Andrew turned onto Interstate 380 and we headed out of town, I realized I'd never left town without an adult before. I felt all grown-up and mature…and excited…and scared…. It wasn't too late to ask Andrew to turn around and take me back home. If I went home right now, my mom would never know that I almost snuck off to Minnesota. But I had to go. I had to find out the truth about my family. So as Andrew picked up speed and the last housing developments whizzed by, I sat back against my seat and settled in for the long ride.

Angela had brought along a deck of cards. We tried to play gin rummy, but the cards kept sliding down the seat. So mostly we played tic-tac-toe and Mad Libs and we took turns with Angela's MP3 player.

We stopped for lunch at a Pizza Hut along the way. Angela and I went to comb our hair and use the bathroom. When we came out, I skidded to a stop. There was a lady dressed in a nurse's outfit standing at the cash register. From the back she looked just like my mom.

"What's the matter?" Angela asked.

"My mom—" I began. When the woman turned around, I breathed a sigh of relief.

"What about your mom?" Angela asked, glancing from me to the woman and back again.

"Nothing," I said, hurrying back to our table.

Angela grabbed my arm. "What do you mean nothing?" She narrowed her eyes at me. "Your mom knows you came with me, doesn't she?"

I didn't answer.

"Doesn't she?" Angela repeated.

"Well…" I chewed my lip. "She'll find out when she gets home from work," I said in a small voice. "I left her a note."

Angela's mouth fell open. "You left her a note?" she screeched. "I thought you said last night you talked to her."

"I did talk to her. It's just…" I looked down at the floor. "Her shower's this weekend. So she said no."

"She said no, but you came anyway? And you *lied* about it to *me?*" Her eyes widened.

Tears welled in my eyes, threatening to spill down my cheeks. I felt shamed. I wasn't just lying to my mom. I was lying to my best friend, too.

"I'm sorry! But this was my only chance to come to Minnesota. I just—"

"What's going on here?" Andrew asked, joining us at the table. He had a plate of bread and salad in his hand. He glanced from one of us to the other.

Please don't tell, I willed Angela. It was bad enough she was mad at me. I didn't want Andrew to know I'd snuck away like some bratty little kid. And I certainly didn't want him to take me back home.

Angela looked at me like she didn't even know me. Finally she shook her head and said, "Nothing." She spun on her heel and went to get some pizza.

The three of us ate in silence. I could feel Andrew

glancing from one of us to the other, wondering what was up. But I kept my head pointed at my plate. I hated having anyone mad at me, but it felt especially bad when it was Angela.

When we finished eating, Andrew drove over to a gas station across the street. Angela bought a magazine of word search puzzles. I got out my book. And for the next half hour it was a silent ride, except for the radio.

I tried to concentrate on my book, but that was hard to do when Angela's anger was taking up the whole back seat. Would she ever speak to me again?

I stared out the window and watched the cornfields go by. I should've told her the truth last night. I should've told her my mom said no.

But would I be on my way to Minnesota right now if I had? Probably not.

We were coming up on the border between Iowa and Minnesota.

"Hey, cool," Andrew said. "The speed limit in Minnesota is 70." He hit the accelerator.

Angela and I glanced toward each other, but then she looked away.

Andrew stuck an old Beatles cassette in the player and cranked the volume. I went back to staring out the window. The countryside was just as dull in southern Minnesota as it was in Iowa. The land was maybe a little flatter. On either side of the road, miles and miles of farmland stretched as far as the eye could see.

"Hey." Angela poked my arm.

"What?" I held my breath. She didn't look quite as mad

as she did earlier, but she didn't look like she'd forgiven me, either.

"I understand why you lied," Angela said carefully. "You were desperate. People who are desperate do desperate things."

I couldn't argue with that.

"You never would have lied to me about anything else. At least, I don't think you would have."

I shook my head. I definitely wouldn't have lied to her about anything else.

"It's just that ever since you started this with your dad, you're like a whole different person."

"No I'm not."

"Yes you are. You're so obsessed. And, well, don't take this the wrong way, Sam…" She shifted in her seat. She seemed to be searching for just the right way to say it. "As your best friend, I have to tell you you're sort of gullible. I mean, you believe everything. You fall for stuff that ordinary people don't fall for."

"I do not!"

"You do too!"

I shook my head. "Maybe it looks that way to you because you're a half-empty kind of person and I'm a half-full kind of person."

Angela tilted her head and frowned at me like I was speaking a foreign language. "What?"

But it made perfect sense to me. "It's how we look at the world," I went on. "You see a glass as half empty. I see the same glass as half full. I'm an optimist. You're a pessimist." It was the main difference between us.

Angela thought about that for a moment. "Maybe," she admitted. "But so what? At least I'm grounded in reality."

"Grounded in reality?" I cried. Then, remembering we weren't alone, I lowered my voice. "You're so grounded in reality, you won't even give your dad a chance. It's like here we are on the way, and you're sitting there like you're expecting your dad to pop up out of nowhere and tell you he changed his mind. You guys can't come after all."

Angela shrugged. "It wouldn't surprise me."

"Nothing surprises you. Nothing bad, anyway."

"That's right. And I can deal with that. But what about you, Sam? What's going to happen when you come face to face with your father and you discover he's not the knight in shining armor you think he is?"

"I don't know," I said honestly. What else could I say?

I had to find out the truth. It was more important to me than anything else. More important than missing my mom's shower, more important than lying to Angela, and more important than what was going to happen to me if it turned out I was wrong about all this.

If my sister was really still alive and living with my dad, one way or another I was going to track them down.

Chapter Thirteen

Andrew turned the music off as we started down the hill into Hill Valley. "You guys awake?" he asked. "We're almost there."

"We're awake," Angela said. She sat up a little straighter and stared out the window.

"So this is where you used to live," I said. We passed a school, then a row of fast-food places and a park. "Looks like a nice town."

No response.

I tapped Angela on the shoulder. "You okay?"

"Yeah," she said, her forehead pressed against the window. "It's just weird to be back. Everything looks so different."

"Tell me about it," Andrew said. I have to say I was really impressed that he never once needed Angela to check the map the whole trip.

"Have you guys been to your father's house before?" I asked.

Angela snorted. "We used to live there."

"Oh." She'd never told me her dad lived in her old house.

"Dad bought Mom out when we moved to Iowa," Andrew explained.

We turned onto a nice tree-lined street. The houses were bigger than my house, but not huge. And not fancy. They were just regular nice houses. Bikes and scooters rested in front of several of them.

Andrew stopped in front of a tall white house with red trim. A large porch stretched across the whole front of the house. A red ball, a plastic shovel, and a little yellow dump truck lay in the front yard.

It had been three hours since we'd stopped at Pizza Hut, so I was pretty anxious to get out of the car and stretch, not to mention go to the bathroom. But Angela and Andrew took their sweet time getting out of the car. They both stared at the house as though they'd never seen it before.

"What's the matter?" I asked, glancing over at the house. I didn't see anything out of the ordinary.

"Our house is supposed to be blue," Angela said, slamming her car door.

"It's been a while since we've been here," Andrew said. "I'm sure this isn't the only thing that's changed."

The door to the house swung open and a little boy with curly blond hair toddled out onto the porch and grinned. A woman with matching curly hair followed close behind. She reminded me of a toy poodle, kind of small and nervous.

"Well, hello there." She scooped up the little boy in her arms and clomped down the stairs to greet us. "You made it." I noticed her smile was a little too big for her mouth.

"Hi, Noreen," Andrew said. He had a pretty fake smile on his face, too.

Angela didn't say anything.

Noreen carefully set the little boy down on the grass and he toddled over to me. "Baaah?" he said. He had the bluest eyes I'd ever seen.

"Cameron wants you to play ball with him, Angela," Noreen said to me.

What? Did she think I was Angela?

"She's not Angela," Angela spoke right up. "I am. This is my friend, Sam. Remember, I called last night and asked if she could come?"

Angela sort of sidestepped around Cameron, trying not to look at him. But I could tell she was checking him out through the corner of her eye.

"Oh, yes, of course," Noreen said, her cheeks flushed with embarrassment. She came over and shook my hand. "It's nice to meet you, Sam." I noticed I was the only one of the three of us that Noreen touched.

"Goodness, I should've known which one was Angela," Noreen said. "It hasn't been *that* long since we've seen you."

But obviously it had been. Angela and I don't look very much alike. No one who really knew us would ever mistake one for the other.

Angela grabbed my suitcase out of the trunk and handed it to me. "Where's my father?" she asked.

Noreen blinked. "At the hospital." She seemed surprised that Angela didn't know. "He doesn't get home until seven."

"But I thought…never mind," Angela said, shaking her head. She hoisted her suitcase up out of the trunk, then trudged up the front walk.

I knew exactly what she thought. She thought her father would've been here waiting for her.

As soon as we got inside, Andrew pulled out his cell phone and called their mom to let her know they'd arrived safely. I felt a little funny when he did that, like I should be calling my mom to let her know I'd arrived safely, too. But unless I wanted to get yelled at, there was no point in doing that.

When Andrew got off the phone, Noreen showed us all where we would be sleeping. Andrew got the couch in the basement. And Angela and I got a room with blue-and-white flowered wallpaper. There were two twin beds with matching white bedspreads, a night table, and a dresser. Other than that, the room was bare.

"We don't even get my old room," Angela grumbled once Noreen left. "We get the *guest* room. I suppose the kid has my old room."

She marched across the hall and yanked open the door. But that room was obviously a computer room, not a little kid's room.

Angela checked the next room. "Okay. I guess he's got Andrew's old room. That makes sense," she said, her eyes taking in the sailboat wallpaper. "This is a boy's room. But my room…"

She wandered back to the computer room, yet didn't venture inside. It was like there was an electric wire stretched across the threshold. "This room used to be pink." Now it had wood paneling.

Poor Angela. I could only imagine how she felt.

* * *

I jumped when the phone rang.

Angela and I were playing gin rummy in the guest room while we waited for her dad to get home from the hospital.

"I bet that's my father calling to say he's going to be late," Angela said as she discarded a king of hearts.

I didn't think it was Angela's dad on the phone. I had a feeling it was my mom. It was almost five o'clock. Surely she would've gotten my note by now.

But apparently it wasn't either my mom or Angela's dad because nobody ever came to tell either of us we had a phone call. And within about ten minutes, Angela's dad came home.

Angela flew down the stairs.

A guy who I assumed was her father stood at the foot of the stairs with a grocery bag of what smelled like roast chicken. He was taller than I'd pictured him. And very important looking with neatly combed dark hair, a plain white shirt, and a tie.

"Well, look who's here," he said with a stiff smile. He handed the bag to Noreen, then placed each arm awkwardly around Angela and Andrew without really hugging them. Couldn't he see that Angela wanted a real hug? At least he didn't hug Cameron, either. He just sort of ruffled the little boy's hair and said, "Hey, big guy!"

"Dadadadadada!" squealed Cameron.

I guess Mr. Hunter wasn't real big on hugging.

"This is my friend, Sam." Angela introduced us.

"It's nice to meet you, Sam." He shook my hand and practically broke every bone in it, he had such a strong grip.

"Hi," I said as though my hand wasn't killing me at all. "Thanks for letting me come with Angela."

"We're glad you could come," he said formally.

"Let's go sit down before the dinner gets cold." Noreen ushered everyone toward the kitchen and I massaged my sore hand.

I sat next to Angela. Andrew and Cameron sat across from us. Their dad and Noreen sat at opposite ends of the table. Noreen leaned over and turned on the classical music radio station.

Angela and her brother exchanged a look, but I didn't know what it meant.

"Well." Mr. Hunter glanced around the table at Andrew, Angela, and me. "What do you kids think you'll want to do while you're here?"

I knew exactly what I wanted to do!

"There are a lot of things to choose from," Noreen said brightly. "There's swimming, roller-skating, movies…"

"Are you planning to take some time off work while we're here?" Angela asked casually as she passed her father the carton of mashed potatoes.

Mr. Hunter let out a nervous laugh. "Well, I wish I could. But I have patients. You know I can't just leave them."

"Of course not." Angela kicked me under the table, then raised her right eyebrow pointedly.

I didn't know what to say or do in response.

"I figured you'd both want to see all your old friends

while you're here," Mr. Hunter said. He turned to Andrew. "I ran into what's-his-name at the grocery store the other day." He glanced over at Noreen. "What *is* his name?"

Noreen was tearing a roll apart for Cameron. "You mean the Slater boy? Brian?"

"That's right. Brian. He's working at Rainbow Foods now. I told him you were coming up this week, Andrew. He said he'd love to see you."

"Cool," Andrew replied, shoving a forkful of potatoes into his mouth. "I can show him my car."

"And I'd be happy to drop you girls off anywhere you'd like to go," Noreen said. "As long as you're willing to plan around Cameron's nap."

Ha! I wondered whether she'd be willing to "drop us off" in front of 7430 Sheridan Avenue South in Richland?

Later, when Angela and I were getting ready for bed in the guest room, Angela said, "I don't know why my dad even agreed to let us come up here if he isn't going to spend any time with us."

"Maybe it's like he said. He thought you'd want to see your old friends," I suggested.

Angela pulled her bed spread down. "I was in second grade when we moved away from here," she said. "I don't really have friends here anymore. Besides, I came to see him. Not my old friends."

The phone rang and I stopped breathing. Someone picked it up on the first ring. I didn't move for a full thirty seconds.

Then I relaxed. By then I figured if it was my mom, somebody would've called me.

"Well, if you don't mind," I said, crawling into bed. "I'd like to go to the bus station tomorrow. I want to see if there's a bus to Richland and find out what time it leaves and what time it gets back."

Angela plopped down her bed. "You're really going to go up there? By yourself?"

Was Angela really so surprised? "That's why I came up here," I said. "Well, that and to hang out with you. Do you want to come with me?"

Angela shrugged. "Maybe. It's not like there's anything better to do around here. We can walk to the bus station. It's just a few blocks away. How much do you think a bus ticket would cost?"

Before I could answer, there was a knock at our door.

"Yeah?" Angela called.

Noreen opened the door and poked her head in. "Telephone for you, Sam," she said, handing me a phone. She pinched her lips together in disapproval.

I gulped. Uh oh.

Noreen left, closing the door softly behind her. Angela gave me an I'm-glad-I'm-not-you look, then grabbed the headphones for her MP3 player and put them on.

I slowly raised the phone to my ear, gripping it with both hands. "H-hello?" I said shakily.

"You are in big trouble, young lady!"

"Mom, I can explain—"

"Can you? Can you really? Well, start talking, Sam, because I'd love to hear how you ended up in Hill Valley, Minnesota, when I specifically told you you couldn't go."

What? She wanted me to tell her right now?

I gulped again. "Well," I began in a small voice. "I-I can't tell you right now. But I promise I'll tell you when I get back to Clearwater—"

"That's going to be sooner than you think," Mom spat at me. "I already spoke with Angela's stepmother. They'll take you to the bus station tomorrow morning and you're going to be on the eight-twenty bus to Cedar Rapids. I'll have to leave work a few minutes early, but I'll be in Cedar Rapids when you arrive at three forty-five."

"Mom, no!" I couldn't go home! Not yet! Not until I'd been to Richland.

"Don't 'Mom, no' me. If it wasn't so late, I'd drive up there and get you myself right now. Unfortunately it took a while to get a hold of Anne to find out where you were. I noticed your cell phone is conveniently turned off. Funny, Anne was under the impression you had permission to go to Minnesota. She was pretty surprised to find out otherwise."

I couldn't worry about what Angela's mom thought of me right now. "Mom, you have to let me stay—" I begged. I never in a million years thought she'd make me go home.

"You're not staying, Sam! You're going to get on that bus in the morning and come home. And it'll be a long time before you even think about going anywhere else."

Chapter Fourteen

The first thing I noticed about the Hill Valley bus station the next morning was the smell. The whole place smelled like fried eggs. But even though I hadn't eaten anything that morning, I didn't feel at all hungry.

I shuffled along in line until it was my turn at the ticket counter. "One-way ticket to Cedar Rapids, Iowa," I mumbled to the guy behind the counter. I handed him my mom's debit card.

Angela and her dad waited for me over by the map of Minnesota. They both stared at that map as though it was the most interesting thing in the world.

The ticket guy handed me my mom's card and my ticket. "Your bus is already here. Lane 1. But we won't be boarding for another half an hour. Next?"

I picked up my ticket, then moped over to Angela and her dad. *It was over.* I was heading home with no more information than I'd come with. Plus I was going to see some major trouble when I got there. Probably more trouble than I'd ever seen before in my entire life.

Angela's dad smiled uncomfortably. He checked his watch. "You don't need me to wait around until the bus leaves, do you?" he asked. "I really should be getting in to the hospital."

"Oh, no," I said right away. Something about Angela's dad made me want to stand at attention. "I have my ticket." I held it up. "The bus is here. I'll be fine."

Angela's dad looked relieved. "Okay, then," he said, holding out his hand. "It was nice meeting you, Sam. I hope you have a nice ride back home."

"Thanks," I said as he about killed my hand again.

He started to walk away when Angela called out, "Wait! Don't I get to say good-bye to Sam before we leave?"

He turned and glanced quizzically at his daughter. "We?"

"Well, yeah," Angela's voice dropped. "Aren't you going to drop me off back at…your house before you go to the hospital?"

Her dad laughed. "Angela, the house is only a few blocks from here. I think you can walk." Then he turned right back around and headed out to the parking lot like the busy, important man that he probably was.

I guess I didn't think it was *that* big of a deal. Angela and I had talked about walking here by ourselves last night. But Angela was ticked. "It would serve him right if I got mugged walking back by myself," she grumbled.

"In this town?" I cried. Hill Valley wasn't any bigger than Clearwater.

"It happens," Angela said.

There was no place to sit down in the bus station except at the breakfast counter. And it didn't seem right to sit there if we weren't going to eat anything. So we wandered outside.

It smelled even worse out here. Diesel fuel.

Another bus was just pulling in. It said Mall of America in the little screen above the driver. I knew the Mall of America was near Minneapolis. I wondered how far it was from Richland.

Angela leaned back against the brick building and sighed. "I ought to just hop on that bus and go to the Mall of America today," she said.

I sighed. "Me, too. I'm already in trouble. What's a little more?"

Angela she looked at me. "I could do it if I wanted to. My dad gave me eighty bucks this morning. He told me to go to the mall and buy myself something nice. On him." She snorted.

Whoa! Eighty bucks? "So, do it," I said with a shrug.

"Go to the Mall of America?" Angela asked. "Without permission?"

"No," I laughed. "Go to the mall here and buy yourself something nice."

"Oh. Right." Angela nodded knowingly. Then she raised her eyebrow at me. "You don't think I'd do it, do you?"

"Do what?"

"Get on that bus and go to the Mall of America."

Uh, no. There was no way Angela would do that. She was the responsible one. I was the crazy one.

Angela shrugged. "Why don't you go in there," she tilted her head toward the bus station, "and see if you can find out how to get where you want to go in Richland from the Mall of America."

My eyes about popped out of my head when she said that.

"What?" Angela said with a shrug. "I thought that was why you came up here. You wanted to go see if this guy in Richland is your dad and find out whether he has your sister." I saw a mischievous look in Angela's eyes that I'd never seen there before.

"Well, I do, but…" But what? There was no one here to make sure I got on the right bus. And like I'd just told Angela, I was already in a heap of trouble. What was a little more? Especially if I found my dad and my sister.

So we hurried back inside to talk to the guy at the ticket counter. It turned out the Mall of America bus just went to the Mall of America. But we could catch a city bus there that would take us over to Penn Avenue. We'd stay on the city bus until we got to 74th Street. Then we'd walk three blocks to Sheridan Avenue and we'd be there. Piece of cake.

Angela and I looked at each other and grinned.

"What do you think?" Angela asked.

"Let's do it!" I said.

I half-expected the ticket guy to refuse to let me change my ticket without a parent's permission. But there hadn't been a parent standing there when I'd bought the ticket in the first place. So no problem. I changed my one-way ticket to Cedar Rapids to a round-trip ticket to the Mall of America. And Angela bought another round-trip ticket to the Mall of America. We'd arrive at eleven-thirty and get back at nine o'clock tonight.

"My dad's going to kill me when we get back," Angela said with a huge smile on her face.

"And my mom's going to kill me," I said. But for some reason, that didn't really bother me at the moment.

As the bus to Cedar Rapids pulled away without me, I picked up my cell phone and dialed the hospital where my mom worked. "Hi, this is Samantha Wright," I said when the receptionist picked up the phone. "I'm Suzanne Sperling's daughter. Could you please tell her not to pick me up in Cedar Rapids? Tell her I'm not on the bus."

"Anything else, Samantha?" the woman asked in a bored voice.

"No, that'll do it," I said. Then I snapped my cell phone closed and hit the power button.

"The bus to Mall of America is now boarding in lane 3," a voice came over the intercom.

Angela and I looked at each other and giggled. I didn't know about Angela, but I felt like a wild animal escaping from the zoo. Giddy with excitement, we grabbed hands, ran outside, and climbed onto the bus.

* * *

The bus stopped in every piddly town between Hill Valley and the Mall of America. In fact, some of the places we stopped were so small I could hardly believe they really were towns. All the starting and stopping—plus the bus fumes and the perfume of the lady in front of us—made my stomach feel queasy.

Angela nudged me. "You don't look so good, Sam. Are you okay?"

"I think I'm bus sick," I moaned, clutching my stomach.

"Open the window."

"Are you kidding?" I cried. "That would totally mess up my hair."

"Hey, better to have messy hair than smell like puke," Angela said.

She had a point. I cracked the window and a cool blast of fresh air hit me right in the nose. Every time a wave of nausea came over me, I stuck my nose in the crack of open window and inhaled deep breaths of fresh air until I felt better. When we reached the outskirts of the Twin Cities there was enough traffic around us that the air outside the bus probably wasn't much fresher than the air inside the bus. But I did manage to make it all the way to the Mall of America without throwing up.

Wow! Angela and I knew the mall would be big, but we had no idea it was *this* big. All we could do was stare at it in awe. You have to understand, for two girls from Iowa, the Mall of America was mind-boggling. More than five hundred stores under one roof?

The bus let us out on the lowest level of a big parking ramp. The guy I talked to at the Hill Valley bus station said we'd be able to see where the city buses picked up when we got off the Hill Valley bus. And sure enough, there they were across the parking lot. But I wasn't sure I was ready to go over there and get on the next bus. I wasn't sure I was ready to face whatever I might find at 7430 Sheridan Avenue South.

But Angela was already halfway across the parking ramp. She turned when she realized I wasn't with her. "What's the matter?" she asked. "Don't you want to do this?"

I blinked. "Of course I do," I said, hurrying to catch up with her. This was why I was here.

We went down the line checking for the Penn Avenue bus. "This is it," Angela said, stopping in front of a big white bus.

The door opened and we climbed on. "Are you going to Penn Avenue?" Angela asked the bus driver.

He was an old guy with dark skin, glasses, and clumps of white hair that looked like pieces of cotton stuck to the sides of head. He didn't answer out loud, just nodded once.

We dropped our money in the slot, then found a seat in the middle of the bus. We weren't even moving yet, but already I felt bus sick. I wiped my sweaty palms on my shorts and leaned my head back against my seat.

"So, what's the plan?" Angela crossed one leg over the other. "We'll just go up to that house, ring the bell, and see what happens?"

"Pretty much."

"What if nobody answers the door?"

"I don't know."

As the bus started out across the Mall of America parking lot, my stomach heaved.

"Okay, what if someone does answer the door?" Angela persisted. "What then?"

"I don't know!" I wasn't in the mood to talk. I just wanted to rest my head against the hard seat and think. Because believe me, those questions and more were swirling around in my head.

I was starting to have some major doubts about this whole thing. Let's get real. Running off to Minnesota without my mom's permission? Getting on the Mall of America bus instead of the Cedar Rapids bus? Taking another bus across town to a total stranger's house?

What was I thinking?

I turned to the window. There was so much traffic here. So many cars, so many horns. So many buildings. So many people. And here we were, two girls alone in a big city. We could get hit by a car or something up here and no one would ever know because no one even knew we were here. Unlike Clearwater or Hill Valley, there were real dangers in a place like Minneapolis.

But then I thought back to that voice on the answering machine and my hairs stood on end once more. That was my dad's voice on that machine. I was sure of it. And I was pretty sure my sister was still alive.

I had come a long way to find out the truth. So when I saw the sign for 74th Street, I reached up and pulled the cord above the window. A bell rang and the bus slowed.

Was I ready for this?

By the time the bus finally stopped, we were up to 72nd Street.

"We're going to have to walk back a couple blocks, then cut over to Sheridan Avenue," Angela said.

"I know." I didn't care. I needed the few extra minutes to calm myself down.

Angela peered at me. "Are you okay?" she asked as cars whizzed past on the street.

I shrugged. "I'm scared," I said in a small voice.

Angela took my hand. "I don't blame you," she said. "But remember, you're a half-full kind of person. Whatever happens, you should be able to handle it."

It occurred to me that this was all just a big adventure to Angela. She was away from home. Away from her dad. She didn't know whether I was right about my dad living at 7430 Sheridan Avenue South and my sister possibly living there, too. But she was willing to come along and find out.

Me, I was pretty sure I was right. But what if I was wrong?

We crossed the street, then started up 74th Street. The houses around here were small and sad looking. There were no flowers out front. Just lots of scraggly bushes, an occasional big, ugly pine tree, and patches of dead grass. A couple of the houses had cracked windows. Many of them needed paint. Did my dad *really* live around here? Or had he up until a few days ago?

There was a cemetery up ahead. I hated cemeteries. Why would anyone want to live so close to a cemetery?

"I don't think this street goes all the way through," Angela said. "Should we turn here and see if we can get to Sheridan Avenue going this way?"

"Okay," I said. So we made one turn, then another. Finally we came to Sheridan Avenue. Sweat dribbled down my back. My stomach felt funny again.

At least the houses looked a little better along here. They were still small, but they looked more like our little house back in Clearwater. The grass even seemed greener down here and a few houses had flowers out front.

"It shouldn't be much farther," Angela said. "What's the number again?"

"7430."

There were only two houses on this side of the street,

then a playground and what looked like an elementary school. But across the street there was 7418...7424. And then 7430.

I stopped. It was just an ordinary brown house with a big picture window and two tiny bedroom windows. A huge tree towered over it.

"You sure this is it?" Angela asked.

I opened my mouth, but no words came out.

Angela grabbed my arm. "Well, let's go ring the bell and see what happens."

I don't know how I even made it across the street. You know how when you stare at something too hard, the whole image sort of melts apart? That's what was happening to me. Plus my arms and legs were so tingly that I didn't think I could walk. But somehow I found myself standing at the front door.

"Go ahead. Ring the bell," Angela said.

My heart raced. My stomach lurched. I was in serious danger of throwing up. But I stuck out a shaky finger and pressed the button. I heard the bell ring inside the house and a dog came running to the door.

That was unexpected!

"Someone lives here," Angela said.

"Someone with a dog," I added.

The dog scratched at the door and barked at us. But no one yelled at him to stop and no one came to the door.

A fuzzy memory popped into my head. My mom and dad arguing.

"Come on, Suzanne. It's just a dog."

"I don't want a dog. Dogs are too much responsibility."

Angela lifted the top on the black mailbox beside the front door.

"What are you doing?" I asked.

"Checking to see whether Joseph Wright really does live here and whether he's picked up his mail recently."

There was some mail in the box, but not a lot. Two ads from JCPenney and Home Depot. And a couple of bills. All of it addressed to Joseph Wright. There was definitely a Joseph Wright living here. Did Sarah live here, too?

"What should we do?" Angela asked.

Now that I knew for sure he was here, I had to see him. "Wait, I guess," I said.

"He's probably at work," Angela said.

"Probably," I agreed. "Hopefully he works an early shift somewhere and gets off mid-afternoon."

We walked over to the playground across the street and plopped down on the merry-go-round where we had a good view of the house. If anyone came in or out, we would see them.

I had to admit it got a little boring just sitting there. Not to mention hot. But what did I expect? It was the beginning of August. I was determined to wait it out. My dad or Joseph—I wasn't sure what to call him—would come back eventually. And I wanted to be there when he did.

I ran my fingers through my hair. Oh no! After two bus rides and an hour or so sitting in the hot sun, my hair was probably a disaster! I *so* wanted to look good the first time I met my dad. So I whipped out my comb and gently pulled it through my hair.

"Your hair's fine," Angela said, rolling her eyes.

"Really?"

"Well, considering we're sitting out here in 85-degree heat, it's probably as good as it's going to get."

"Gee, thanks," I said. I kept right on combing.

It was almost two o'clock. My stomach growled.

"Should we go get something to eat and then come back?" Angela asked.

"I don't want to leave," I said, finally putting my comb away. I knew that if I took my eyes off the house for one second, I'd miss something.

"We'll only be gone for a little bit," Angela said. "Then we'll come right back. And we'll ring the doorbell again, in case we missed him."

I shook my head. "You go if you want. I'm staying here."

"Well, I don't think we should split up," Angela said. So we stayed where we were.

After a while, Angela got up and started walking around. "I have to go to the bathroom," she said. "Do you?"

I did. Kind of. But I still didn't want to leave. "I'm okay."

I noticed there was a door open at the school. "You could probably use the bathroom in there," I told Angela.

She glanced at the open door, then back at me. "Okay. You sure you don't want to come with me?"

"Nah." I shook my head again.

But once she was gone, I wished I had gone with her. It was kind of creepy sitting there by myself. I could hear birds chirping and wind rustling through the trees. There was absolutely nobody around.

I felt better when Angela came back. She held out two

bags from Taco Bell. One had food in it, the other drinks.

"Where'd you get that?" I asked.

"Over there." She pointed to a busier street on the other side of the school. "Across the street."

We were so hungry we gobbled up the tacos and nachos in about two minutes flat. And of course after I drank the pop I really had to go to the bathroom. I knew I could run into that school like Angela did, but I didn't want to. I was sure that the minute I left, my dad would come home. So I crossed my legs and tried not to think about it.

Angela checked her watch. "We're going to have to head back to the Mall of America in an hour or so. We don't want to miss the bus back to Hill Valley."

I didn't say anything. She was right, of course. But how could I leave if my dad hadn't come back yet?

"Sam? Did you hear what I said?"

"Yes!"

"I mean, this has been fun and everything, but we don't want to be stuck here all night. If this guy hasn't come back by five-thirty, we have to leave."

"I know!" I said. To tell you the truth, though, I wasn't sure I would be willing to leave at five-thirty. Not if my dad hadn't come back.

Before I could argue the point any further, I noticed this person around my age coming toward us. I say person because the whitish blond hair was cropped so short I honestly couldn't tell whether it was a boy or a girl. But as the person drew closer, I could tell it was definitely a girl because she had…well, she had breasts.

She wore a softball uniform and carried an equipment bag. There was a smudge of dirt on her cheek. All of a sudden, goosebumps dotted my arms and the back of my neck.

I can't explain it, but I just knew.

"Sarah?"

I didn't even realize I'd spoken out loud until the girl turned and looked at me.

Then I knew for sure. "Oh my God!" I gasped. "You really are alive."

Chapter Fifteen

The girl looked at me like I had three heads. "Huh?"

I moved toward her. "You're Sarah, right?" I said.

"No." The girl shook her head. "My name's T. J." She glowered at me, chomping on a big wad of strawberry bubblegum.

T. J.? No! She was Sarah. She had to be. We were about the same age. Same height. We had the exact same shade of whitish blond hair. She wore her hair totally different than I wore mine. She wore it totally different than I ever *would* wear mine. But...she was Sarah. She had to be.

Angela grabbed my arm. "I don't think this girl is your sister, Sam," she said. "She looks too—" Angela looked the girl up and down. "She's too *not like you* to be your sister."

The girl snorted. "I don't have a sister," she said as she started to walk away.

"But—" I wiggled out of Angela's grasp and started after the other girl. She looked annoyed to find me walking beside her, staring at her face. She had kind of a tomboyish look about her. There wasn't a single speck of makeup on her face at all. But aside from that, I was sure I saw a resemblance between us.

Okay, maybe we didn't look exactly alike, but we were definitely related. That much was obvious. Hey, maybe we were fraternal twins rather than identical twins. Didn't she see it too?

"You turned when I said Sarah," I said to the girl. Didn't that mean something?

She looked at me like yeah, so?

"You did!" I insisted.

"She turned because you were talking to her," Angela said as though I were a five-year-old. "You'd turn too if you were walking across the park and someone started talking to you."

She smiled nervously at T. J. "Sorry we bothered you," she said as she tried to lead me away.

"Sure." The girl shrugged like I was just another nutcase, then continued across the park.

She wasn't Sarah.

I looked at Angela. "I was so sure."

"I know."

"No, really," I said. "The moment I saw that girl…" She was almost to the street now. "I just—I don't know. I felt a connection."

"You wanted her to be your sister," Angela said soothingly. "You wanted it to be true, so you thought you felt something when you really didn't."

But I *did* feel something. Even now, watching her cross the street, I still felt it. That girl was my sister. Didn't she feel it, too? A connection to me? Why didn't she look back?

"Come on." Angela touched my arm. "We should head back to the Mall of America."

My eyes were glued to the girl's back. Where was she going?

She was going to my dad's house!

"Hey!" I yelled, running after her. "Wait a minute!"

"Sam!" Angela cried.

The girl turned as I barreled across the street. She had the screen door open and was about to insert a key in the lock when I came running up behind her.

"You live here?" I gasped, struggling to catch my breath.

She looked at me like what-are-you-babbling-about-now, like I was some pesky mosquito that wouldn't go away.

"Is your last name Wright?" I tried again. "Is Joseph Wright your dad?"

She let the screen door close, then planted a hand on her hip. "Who are you?" she asked.

Her eyes were exactly the same shade of green as mine. She also had a pointy nose. Just like mine. And her right ear was pierced two times while her left ear was pierced just once. Talk about weird. That was exactly how my ears were pierced.

She had a mole on the left side of her chin. I had one on the right side of mine.

"Come on, Sam! You can't just—" Angela screeched to a halt beside me. Her eyes darted back and forth between me and the other girl, whoever she was. Then she frowned. "You know, you guys do look kind of alike."

Kind of? If I chopped off most of my hair off to look

like hers, we would look like *twins*. I could tell by the confusion in the other girl's eyes that she saw it now, too.

"Who are you?" she asked again.

"I'm Sam," I said as though that explained it all.

She looked at me blankly. "Sam who?"

"Samantha Wright."

Still no reaction.

"Doesn't that name mean anything to you?" I asked.

She shrugged. "Not really."

I didn't get it. How could she totally forget me?

"Is your last name Wright?" I asked.

"Yes."

"And is your dad's name Joseph Wright?"

"Yes."

"Joseph Wright is my dad!" I said.

She didn't look convinced.

"I heard his voice on your answering machine. It's him! I know it is!" Speaking of answering machines...and disconnected phones... "Why is your phone disconnected?"

She frowned. "It's not."

"Yes, it is. I called and left a message on your answering machine. But when I called back, the phone had been disconnected."

"Our phone number got changed—"

Aha! "Why?"

"I don't know. Ask the phone company." She looked at me like quit-bugging-me, but I couldn't stop now.

"You're my sister. My *twin* sister. Can't you tell? We have the same eyes and the same nose and we even pierced our ears the same way!"

"Easy, Sam," Angela said. "You're freaking her out."

I was. The girl, Sarah or T. J. or whoever she was, looked nervous. Which was funny because I could tell she was the kind of girl who didn't take crap from anyone. The kind of girl who punched first and asked questions later. The kind of girl who was very different from me.

Angela stepped up to the girl and stuck out her hand. "Hi," she said with a smile. "I'm Angela, Sam's friend."

The girl shook Angela's hand weakly, but didn't smile.

"We could probably clear this whole thing up really quick if you had a photo of your dad or something," Angela went on. "Something so Sam can see for sure whether she's got the right Joseph Wright."

"I know I've got the right one," I insisted. I could not take my eyes off the girl. "And I also know…you're my sister."

"Well, let her get a picture anyway," Angela said. "Just to be sure. Do you have a picture?" she asked T. J.

"Yes," T. J. replied. She was sort of checking me out, too. "But I'll tell you one thing. If Joe really is your dad, then there's no way I could be your sister."

"How do you know?"

"Because he's not my real dad."

"He isn't?" Angela and I said at the same time.

"No." She shook her head. "Not that it's any of your business. Sometimes people think he's my dad because we have the same blond hair. But Joe was my real dad's best friend. He adopted me when my parents died."

"Your parents died?" I repeated. This wasn't making any sense.

"They died when I was little. I don't really remember them."

"Did you ever have a sister?" I asked desperately.

T. J. blew a bubble with her gum, then sucked it back in. "No. I had a brother. An older brother. But he died when my parents did."

"I'm sorry," Angela said.

T. J. shrugged. "Like I said, I don't really remember them. It was a long time ago. What makes you think Joe is your dad?"

I launched into the whole story, beginning with the psychic and the newspaper clippings and ending with the disconnected phone. I had to admit, the whole thing sounded pretty lame when I said it out loud.

"So…when you saw me, you thought I was your sister?" T. J. asked. She clearly wasn't buying it.

"Well—"

"Look, I'll get you that picture," T. J. said abruptly. "You can at least see if Joe is your dad. But if he's not, I want you to leave, okay? This is just too bizarre."

"Okay," I agreed. That was all I really wanted anyway.

Angela and I stayed on the driveway while T. J. turned back to her house. As soon as she pulled the screen door open, the dog started barking. "Hang on, Sherlock! I'm coming."

Both Angela and I whipped our heads around. "Sherlock?" I ran toward her. "Your dog's name is Sherlock?"

T. J. grinned. "Yeah." She opened the door and this

shaggy mass of white fur leaped at her legs. T. J. bent down and picked him up. His whole hind end wiggled in her arms and he licked her neck.

"Isn't he the greatest?" T. J. asked, bringing the dog over to me so I could pet him. "He's a West Highland terrier."

I gave the dog an obligatory pat on the head.

"We got him when he was just a pup and he was so nosy! Into everything. That's why we named him Sherlock."

"My cat's name is Sherlock," I said.

T. J.'s smile froze to her face. "What?"

"It's true," Angela said. She could vouch for me.

"I got him when I was ten. I named him after Sherlock Holmes."

"That's…weird," T. J. said, hugging her dog close to her chest. I could tell she didn't like it that our pets had the same name.

"It's really weird," Angela said.

T. J. bit her bottom lip like she was debating whether or not to say something. She took a step closer to me. "You want to hear something that's even weirder?" she asked.

I swallowed hard. "What?"

T. J. hesitated for just a second. "Your name is Sam, right?"

"Well, my real name is Samantha. But everyone calls me Sam."

T. J.'s eyes locked on mine and she said, "My brother? The one who died? His name was Sam, too."

Chapter Sixteen

I shivered. T. J. didn't remember ever having a sister, but she had a brother named Sam who died? How creepy was that?

"When's your birthday?" I asked, shifting my weight from one foot to the other. We were still standing out in T. J.'s driveway.

T. J. eyed me warily. "August 26," she replied.

Okay, that proved it. We had to be twins!

"That's my birthday, too!" I told her excitedly. You're going to be fourteen, right?"

T. J. shook her head. "Thirteen," she said, chomping her gum.

I blinked. "Thirteen? You mean you're only twelve now?"

She nodded.

That couldn't be right.

"What grade are you going into?" Angela asked.

"Eighth."

And I was going into ninth. "But we have the same birthday," I protested. "The same birthday, same hair color, same eye color, same pet names, same dad—" Even though he was her *adopted* dad.

"But T. J.'s a year younger than you," Angela pointed out. "And she's adopted. And we haven't actually seen a picture of this guy yet. We don't know for sure that he's your dad."

T. J. looked as uneasy as I felt. "Why don't you guys come in and I'll get that picture of Joe."

"Y-you call him Joe?" I asked.

She hesitated. "That's his name. Come on." T. J. put the dog down and opened the front door. The little dog scampered into the house, his tail wagging the whole way. Angela and I followed close behind.

It was warm in the house. T. J. and Joe didn't have air conditioning. But despite the heat, I felt chilled just being inside their house. *My dad's house.* This was where he got up every morning, had breakfast, went to work, came home, had dinner, watched TV, and did whatever else he did.

The house looked totally different from our house. It had what you'd call that "lived-in" look. None of the furniture matched. There was an old caramel-colored couch that was piled with newspapers, a couple of scratched-up tables (one of them had a dirty glass on it), and a green wooden rocker. There was a picture of a group of dogs playing band instruments hanging on the wall. I couldn't imagine any of this stuff in our house. Or in Bob's house, for that matter.

T. J. opened a closet and pulled a photo album down from the shelf. "Okay," she said, opening it up. "This is Joe." She pointed.

I peered over her shoulder and saw a photo of a man raking leaves. He looked older than the guy in those newspaper articles I'd found in our basement, but I recognized the hair, the eyes, the mustache. He used to tickle me with that mustache!

"That's him!" I cried, drawing in my breath. "That's my dad."

T. J. stiffened.

"Are you sure?" Angela asked.

"Positive." Too bad I didn't have that photo from the newspaper article to prove it. But I did have another one. I opened my purse and took out the photo of Sarah and me that I'd taken from that same box.

"Look at this," I said, handing T. J. the photo.

She looked at it so hard she practically burned a hole in it. She even stopped chewing her gum.

I could hardly breathe. "Is one of those girls you?"

T. J. didn't take her eyes off the photo. "I don't know," she said softly.

"What do you mean you don't know?" I asked. "How can you not know whether a photo is you or not?" Of course, I wasn't sure which one was me, either.

"Let's compare it to a photo you have of yourself when you were little," Angela suggested.

"That's just it," T. J. said, raising her eyes to meet mine. "I don't have any photos of me from when I was little."

"You don't?"

She shook her head. "They all got burned in the fire."

"What fire?"

"The fire that killed my parents and my brother."

I chewed my bottom lip. I didn't know what to think anymore. There were so many coincidences. But so many other things didn't quite add up.

"Where did you live with your parents and your brother?" I asked. "Did you live in Iowa?"

"Yes," T. J. said, surprised. "I was born in a town called Clearwater."

"That's where I live!" I cried.

T. J. and I just stared at one another in amazement. I'm not sure either one of us took a breath.

I cleared my throat. "When will…" I didn't know what to say. Your dad? My dad? Our dad? "When will Joe be home?" I said finally. Joe was what she called him. He was the key to this whole thing. The one who could answer all our questions.

"I don't know." She glanced at the little round clock on the wall above the kitchen table. "Before last week, he probably would've been home by now. He's a handyman, so he just works a couple hours here and a couple hours there. Whenever he's got a job, I mean. But he hasn't been home much lately because Gram's been pretty sick—"

Gram? Did she mean Grandma Wright?

"She's in a nursing home," T. J. went on. "And she's not doing very well. Joe just got a job this week, too. So he's been splitting his time between the job and the nursing home. He hasn't been coming home until like nine or ten o'clock at night."

"Nine or ten at night?" Angela repeated. "We can't hang around that long. We have to get back to Hill Valley,

Sam. She checked her watch, "In fact, if we don't leave soon, we're going to miss the bus!"

The last thing on my mind was catching a bus back to Hill Valley.

"I can't leave," I said. "Not until I see my dad."

"I know," Angela said. "But Sam, that's the only bus back to Hill Valley tonight. If we're not on it, how are we going to get back?"

"Maybe I should call Joe's cell phone and tell him I need him to come home," T. J. offered. She still looked a little unsure about all this.

"Could you?" I asked. As far as I was concerned, the sooner he got here, the better.

"He only wants me to call if it's an emergency," T. J. explained. "But this is sort of an emergency."

"Go call," Angela said. "If Sam and I aren't on that last bus to Hill Valley, it will definitely be an emergency!"

So T. J. went into the kitchen to make her call. Angela and I just stood around in the living room.

"What do you think?" I whispered. "Do you think she's Sarah?"

"I don't know," Angela whispered back. "I didn't at first, but now? I don't know."

I paced back and forth. I couldn't stand still. "What makes you think it's possible?" I asked. "The fact that we look so much alike? Or that she doesn't have any pictures from when she was little? Or that she was born in Clearwater? Or that we have the same birthday?"

"I don't know. All of that together, I guess."

"I couldn't get ahold of him," T. J. said as she came back into the living room. "I left a message with his answering service, though. He'll come home as soon as he gets the message."

"What'd you say in the message?" I asked. Would she have just come right out and said, *"Hey, Joe. Your other daughter is here"?* And what would his reaction be? After all, if this was true—if T. J. was Sarah—then I was the daughter he'd left behind. The one he didn't want.

Why didn't he want me?

"I didn't really say anything. I just said there was a family emergency and I needed him to come home. He'll probably think it's about Gram."

My head was spinning. Grandma Wright. Dad. Sarah. T. J. It was all too much. What was going on here? What happened all those years ago?

"Should we wait in my room?" T. J. asked.

"Sure," Angela said.

"Why not," I said. So we followed T. J. down the hall. Sherlock plodded along behind us, his nose to the floor.

I couldn't help but look in all the rooms we passed along the way—the paneled TV room, the small bathroom, Joe's bedroom…I lingered in the doorway there. This was where my dad slept.

The window shades were pulled and there was paneling on the walls in here too, only this paneling was darker than the stuff in the other room. It was so dark you could go to sleep right in the middle of the day. I spotted a single unmade bed against one wall and a banged-up old dresser against another. A ceiling fan hummed as it spun above.

But there was nothing on the walls. Nothing that told me who this Joe Wright was or what was important to him.

"Are you coming?" T. J. poked her head out of her room and looked at me.

"Yeah." I pulled myself away from my dad's room.

When I got to T. J.'s room, I thought I was in a boy's room. There were tons of sports posters on the wall. Most of the people looked like baseball players, but there was at least one basketball player, too. I didn't even know who half those people were.

"I guess you like sports, huh?" Angela said as we both sat down on the navy comforter. T. J. pulled out her desk chair and straddled it backwards, her arms resting on the top of the chair back.

"Yeah. Joe and I are into all kinds of sports."

Didn't she like any movie stars or singers? And what about pictures of her friends? She didn't even have a mirror above her dresser to stick pictures of her friends in like I did. How did she do her makeup and hair without a mirror?

Speaking of hair, no doubt mine looked terrible. And I was about to meet my dad for the very first time.

I hopped up. "Do you have a curling iron I could borrow real quick?" I asked T. J. Hopefully I had time to do something with my hair before my dad got here.

"No," she said.

I frowned. "You don't have one that you're willing to let me borrow?"

"No, I don't have one."

"You don't have a curling iron?" I gaped at her. How could anyone not have a curling iron?

She snorted. "What do I need one for?" she asked, poking at her short, spiky hair. It couldn't have been more than half an inch long anywhere on her head.

Did she always wear her hair so short?

"You look fine, Sam," Angela said in a tired voice. She pulled me back down onto T. J.'s bed.

I knew I did not look fine, but—ugh, I was sitting on something. I reached under me and—whoa!—pulled out a stuffed monkey that looked an awful lot like my monkey back home.

"Hey, where did you get this?" I asked, holding it up.

T. J. grabbed the monkey out of my hands. "My grandma made it," she said, dusting it off. Then she tossed it onto her desk, out of my reach.

"I have one just like it at home."

T. J. frowned. "You couldn't have one *just* like it. I just told you, my grandma made it!"

"It looks the same to me," Angela said.

I heard a voice in my head:

Do you know the monkey man?
The monkey man? The monkey man.
Do you know the monkey man?
Who lives on Hartman Lane...

"Does Joe ever call himself the monkey man?" I asked T. J. "The monkey man?"

"Yeah. You know that song 'Do You Know the Muffin Man'? Does Joe ever sing it as 'Do You Know the Monkey Man'?"

"Joe? Sing?" T. J. snorted. "I don't think I've ever heard him sing."

"Oh," I said, disappointed.

"Do you guys play any sports?" T. J. asked.

"Sam and I both play softball," Angela said.

"Oh yeah? What positions?" T. J. asked, growing more interested.

"I play first base," Angela said.

"What about you?" T. J. looked at me.

"Oh. I'm not very good. They like to keep me out of the way, so I play right field."

Angela rolled her eyes.

"What do you mean 'out of the way'?" T. J. slapped her leg and Sherlock popped his head up. "*I* play right field. Right field is a very important position. You have to have a really good arm to play outfield."

"Sure. Whatever." No way could she convince me Coach Frye put me in right field because of my stellar arm.

The conversation fizzled out there, and T. J. and I just sort of checked each other out without being too obvious about it. Neither one of us really knew what to say. Thank goodness for Angela. Whenever the silences stretched too long, she always came up with something for us to talk about. Like hobbies. Or school.

T. J. and I discovered we both played in band. But I played the flute, she played the tuba. I liked social studies, she liked science. We both hated English, though. Finally, something in common! And she didn't think it was at all strange that I could hate English class and still want to be a writer when I grew up.

"Those books they make us read?" she said, wrinkling her nose. "Bo-ring!"

"No kidding," I said. "I'm going to write way better books than those when I grow up. I'm going to write the kinds of books people actually want to read."

"Oh yeah? What kind of books?"

"Mysteries, of course. What do you want to be when you grow up?"

T. J. sat up a little straighter. "A doctor." She said it like there were no other options.

"Wow."

She shrugged. "I want to make a difference in the world."

"You mean you want to find a cure for cancer or something?" Angela asked.

"Maybe," T. J. mused. "Or maybe I'll do something to help people after they've had a stroke. Some sort of surgery that can make them the way they were before."

"Boy, my mom would love you," I blurted out. But as soon as the words were out of my mouth, I wished I could pull them back in. Because if I was right about all this, then my mom was T. J.'s mom, too. And I could tell by the cloud that passed through T. J.'s eyes that she was thinking the same thing.

"What's she like?" T. J. asked, pulling her legs up under her on the chair. "Your mom, I mean."

"Well…" I looked at Angela. Too bad I didn't have a picture. "How would you describe my mom?

"She's a nurse," Angela said, giving me a jump start.

"That's right," I said. "She started out just working in

the hospital, then she went to night school and became a nurse's aide. And now she's a nurse."

"Yeah, but what's she *like?*" T. J. repeated. "I don't even remember what it's like to have a mom. Joe's great. He's really laid back and lots of fun. But sometimes he forgets important stuff like dentist appointments and school conferences. Of course, he doesn't think things like that are important. In some ways, he's like a big kid. He thinks the fun stuff is what really matters."

That was exactly how Mom described him.

"Sam's mom is definitely not a big kid," Angela said.

"Definitely not," I agreed. "In fact, she's probably the opposite of Joe. She's very serious and responsible. She doesn't know much about having fun."

"Oh, I don't know," Angela said. "She's gotten better since she and Bob got engaged."

"Your mom's engaged?" T. J. asked.

Before I could answer, the front door burst open. We all shut up. "T. J.?" a man's voice called.

Sherlock scampered out from under T. J.'s chair and raced down the hall. "Woof! Woof!"

T. J. looked at me. "Joe's home."

"I figured."

"T. J.?" the voice called again. "Where are you? What's the big emergency?"

He poked his head into T. J.'s room and it was like everything stopped. He looked at me and I looked at him. And nobody said a word.

147

Chapter Seventeen

If I ever had any doubt that this Joseph Wright was my father, that doubt was gone now. He was thinner than I expected. Shorter, too. But other than that, he looked exactly like that photo T. J. had. Exactly like the photo of him and my mom in those old newspaper articles. Except older.

He had the same white blond hair as me and T. J., a long face, and a full mustache. He wore an old white T-shirt that was spotted with flecks of paint and jeans that were so faded they were practically white.

This was my dad! I had waited for this moment for so long and now that it was here, I didn't know what to do. But I got the feeling he didn't know what to do, either.

T. J. broke the silence. "Joe, this is Sam and her friend, Angela. From Iowa." Her voice sounded funny. Like there was something caught in her throat. "Sam thinks you're her dad."

He still didn't say anything. He just stared at me. And I stared back.

"Joe?" T. J. said, her voice rising. Her knuckles were

white from gripping the back of her desk chair so hard.

"H-how did you find us?" Joe asked, his voice cracking.

I opened my mouth, but no words came out. I swallowed hard, then tried again. "A detective," I croaked. "On the Internet."

Joe rubbed his face tiredly, as though he hadn't slept in days. "I don't suppose it was all that hard," he said finally. "I wouldn't have thought anyone was looking for me anymore, so these last few years I haven't exactly tried to hide."

"Hide?" T. J. asked. "W-why would you want to hide?"

Joe glanced around nervously. "Is your mom here?" he asked me.

"She's in Clearwater. She doesn't know I'm here."

His shoulders relaxed a little when I said that. But I couldn't tell what he thought about me being there in his house. Was he happy to see me or not?

"Sam says she had a sister," T. J. said. "She showed me a picture. She thinks I'm the sister she thought was dead. That's not...it's not true, is it?"

Beside me I heard Angela draw in a deep breath.

Joe rubbed the bridge of his nose between his eyebrows, then slumped against the doorjamb. He looked totally defeated.

A thousand questions swirled around in my head, but I couldn't grab one to ask. All I could do was stare wide-eyed at him—this man who was my dad.

"If it's true, then...you'd be my dad, too," T. J. rose up from her chair. There was panic in her eyes. "My *real* dad. But that's not right. My real dad died in a fire. You were my dad's best friend, right?"

Joe let out a long sigh. "No, Teej." He shook his head. "I...I am your real dad."

T. J.'s whole face went white.

"T. J...." Joe went over to her, but she backed away from him. "Let me explain."

"Stop." She held up her hand. "I don't want to hear it. I-I can't deal with this." She pushed past Joe and bolted out of her room. Sherlock dashed after her. A few seconds later we heard the front door open, then slam shut. Sherlock let out a soft whimper.

Joe cocked his head to the little rectangular window above. We could all hear T. J.'s heavy stomps across the yard.

"It's okay," Joe said nervously. "She's just going next door. She's got friends there. David and Nick. They're twins." He smiled ruefully.

I didn't know what to say. I glanced at Angela, but she looked just as uncomfortable as I felt.

Joe rubbed his face again and smiled at me. "So...what do we do now?"

He was asking me?

"Maybe we should go in the other room and talk," he said. "I don't know about you, but I sure could use something to drink."

"Okay," I said, slowly unfolding my legs. Oh my gosh! This was my dad. *I was going to have a real conversation with my dad.*

"Um, I think I'll wait here," Angela said, biting her lip. She pulled out her cell phone. "I should call my dad and let him know where we are."

Uh oh! We were going to miss that last bus back to Hill Valley! But…

"Do you want something to drink?" Joe asked Angela.

"No," she said, shaking her head. "I'm fine." She smiled nervously.

"Okay," he said. Then he turned and walked out of the room.

Angela gestured for me to go, so I hurried after him. Hopefully Angela and her dad would figure out how we would get back to Hill Valley tonight.

My legs were so shaky I wasn't sure they'd hold me up. I did manage to make it to the kitchen, though. It was a small galley-style kitchen with a back door at one end and a table and chairs at the other.

I found my dad resting his elbow on the top of the open refrigerator door, peering inside. "Do you want a Coke?" he asked me.

"Okay." I tried to act casual, like this was no big deal, having a Coke with my dad.

He grabbed two cans from the fridge—a can of Coke and a can of beer—then plopped them on the table. Wow! When he stood next to me, I could see I was almost as tall as he was.

I waited until he motioned for me to sit. Then I pulled out a chair and slowly eased myself into it. He sat down heavily in the chair beside me. Then we just sort of looked at each other. A ceiling fan hummed above us. For a moment, it was the only sound in the room.

"I don't know where to start," he said with a short laugh.

"Me either."

He shook his head. "Look at you. You're all grown up."

I blushed.

"Of course, T. J.'s grown up, too, but that's different. I haven't watched you grow. Whenever I think of you, I still picture that three-year-old kid with the broken front tooth."

I did have a broken front tooth when I was a little kid. I got it from a fall off my tricycle.

"I never meant for it to be like this," he said, shifting in his seat. "I never thought...I never wanted..." His voice trailed off.

"Y-you took my sister," I prompted.

He looked down at his beer. "Yes."

"You took her and you let everyone think she was *dead.*" I didn't get it. This man sitting so close to me, *my dad,* seemed like a regular person. How could he have done this terrible thing?

"You have to understand, Sam. Your mom was taking the two of you away from me. She was heading off to medical school in Florida—"

What?

"My mom never went to medical school." She'd be a doctor if she'd gone to medical school. Not a nurse.

"Well, that was her plan. Ever since I first met her, that was all she talked about. Becoming a doctor."

It was?

T. J. said she wanted to be a doctor. How bizarre was that?

"Then your mom got pregnant and we got married and I thought she'd given up all those big ideas," Joe said. "But she didn't. As soon as her folks moved down to Florida, they started telling her about this great medical school down there and how she could still go if she wanted to. They even said they'd pay for it. And they'd take care of you and T. J. while she was in class. All she had to do was move down there and everything would be set.

"So one day she decided this was what she was going to do. She went to see some hotshot lawyer. She said they were going to write up some paper they wanted me to sign that said it was okay if she took you two out of state. But it wasn't okay. It wasn't okay at all." He held his head in his hands.

"But…" I didn't even know where to begin with the questions. This was so totally different from anything I'd ever heard before. "I always thought you guys got divorced because Sarah died."

Joe pressed his lips together. "Is that what your mother told you?"

"I think so." It was either her or Grandma Sperling. I wasn't sure who now.

"No." He shook his head vehemently. "Your mother wanted a divorce practically the day after we got married."

"She did? Why?"

But then I put it all together. They got married young. *Really* young. And Joe just said she got pregnant and they got married. He didn't say they got married and *then* she got pregnant.

"My mom was pregnant before you guys got married?" I asked, totally shocked.

Hearing the words so bluntly seemed to shock Joe, too.

"Well," he hesitated. "Yeah. I guess that's the way it happened."

I couldn't believe it! My mom, Ms. Responsibility, got herself knocked up? Okay, but what did that have to do with why he took my sister? And he didn't just take her, he *faked her death*. That was worse than kidnapping. It was like...*murder* in a way. Sarah didn't really die, but we all thought she did. Joe didn't actually kill her, but he killed her in our minds. He even gave her a different name.

"So, how did you..." I couldn't even say it out loud. I couldn't say *how did you fake my sister's death.*

"I never planned to take T. J. that day," he said. "It just...happened."

"How?" How did something like that just "happen?" And the other question that gnawed at the back of my brain: *Why did you only take her? Why did you leave me behind? Didn't you want me?*

He took another swallow of beer. "Like I said, your mom was taking you guys away. This was going to be my last chance to see either of you for quite a while. Maybe ever, if your grandparents had their way. So I wanted to do something special. Just the three of us. Go on a picnic or something. But then you came down with the flu."

Yes! I remember that!

"I didn't think you were that sick. I thought you could come, too. But your mom wouldn't hear of it. She let me take T. J., but not you. So T. J. and me, we ended up at that old quarry outside Clearwater. She didn't know what was happening. She just ran up and down the path picking dandelions for your mom. But me, my heart was breaking. All I could do was think about how unfair it was that your mom could take you both away from me, just like that."

"So you decided to…make it look like Sarah died?" I asked, squeezing my hands around my Coke.

"No! I didn't want to take her back to your mom, but I never…I never thought about taking her away. Not at first. I just…I didn't know what to do. So I drove her to my mom's. She was living in Waterloo then. She never thought it was right that your mother could take you both away. She wanted to help me. She said she'd keep T. J. for me and in the morning I should call my lawyer and tell him I wasn't going to sign that paper.

"So I drove back to Clearwater. But instead of going to your mom's, I drove back out to the quarry. I needed to figure out what I was going to say to your mom, how I was going to tell her T. J. wasn't coming home that night and she wasn't going to take you guys to Florida. There was an old canoe lying in some brush. I don't know whose it was. You're not even supposed to go canoeing out there. But it was there, so I put it in the water and just sort of drifted around on the water for a while.

"A little while later, I heard voices. The sound startled me. It startled me so bad I dropped one of the oars. So I jumped in after it. And all of a sudden these people came running. They thought they saw a kid fall in.

"I don't know what I was thinking. It all happened so fast. I just sort of went along and said 'Yes, my little girl fell in the water!' The lady went to get help and her husband tried to get me to come out of the water. But I wouldn't. I just kept diving under and coming back up. I don't know what I was doing.

"By the time the cops got there, I had done such a good job convincing these people that my kid really was in the water that I almost believed it myself.

"Then one of the cops found a kid's life preserver in the canoe. I didn't even know it was there. I told him Sarah had taken it off before she fell in. It was all so easy because everyone believed me. The fire department came out and started a search.

"Someone pulled me out of the water and dried me off. And then pretty soon, your mom showed up. Those folks from that other car told the cops they saw a little girl fall into the water." He closed his eyes as though remembering was too painful. "Everyone kept yelling at me, telling me how stupid it was to take a little girl out in a canoe there, like I didn't know that. People asked me whether I saw the No Swimming and No Boating signs. Your mom started beating on me. Literally. I couldn't believe they all thought I was so stupid. That I would really take a little girl out on that water. But that was exactly what they thought. Every last one of them.

"Of course, your Grandma Wright was in a tizzy," Joe went on. "She didn't know what to do. This wasn't what we planned, but it was too late to go back. The story made news all over Iowa. And she had the kid that everyone was looking for. So the first thing she did was tell everyone that T. J. was you. Then she told one of her friends that her other granddaughter was missing and that she had to come to Clearwater to be with the rest of the family. She asked the friend to take care of T. J. while she was gone."

"What did you tell Sarah—er—T. J. about all of this?" I asked. "Didn't she think it was weird that she never got to go home again? Didn't she think it was weird that people were calling her Sam?"

"Well, she was only three years old. Grandma told her it was a funny game and she should pretend she was you. She always liked to play pretend. She stayed with Grandma's friend until after the search was called off and we had the funeral. Then Grandma thought I'd better get T. J.—er, Sarah—and disappear. Which was pretty easy because your mom wanted a divorce anyway. She was picking up and moving to Florida."

Except she never did!

Why not? Was she so broken up over losing one of her children that she couldn't do it? She couldn't follow her dream of becoming a doctor?

"So what happened after that?" I asked.

"I told T. J. we were going on a little trip. Just her and me. It was hard at first because she missed her mom and she especially missed you."

I smiled, then looked down at my can of pop. I liked that she'd missed me.

"There was a time she thought I called her Tara instead of Sarah and she thought that was a funny joke. She thought it was more pretend. So I kept on calling her Tara Jo instead of Sarah Jo. I realized it was probably a good idea to change her name anyway. And pretty soon Tara Jo got shortened to T. J.

"For the first couple of years, we just drove around the

country. I told her you and your mom had died and we couldn't go back to Iowa. That we were going to have a whole new life. She didn't like it at first, but she got used to it. Grandma sent us money now and then and told us what was going on. As far as the police were concerned, the case was closed. Sarah was dead.

"After a while, when I was sure no one was looking for T. J., we settled down in a small town in southern California. I got a job. Your sister started kindergarten. She started a year late because of all the moving around we did before that."

"That's why she's only going into eighth grade?"

"Yeah. We sort of skipped that first birthday, so when you guys turned five, she thought she was turning four.

"Then we moved to Oregon and South Dakota and finally Minnesota, because my mom had moved here. I found a guy who drew up some fake adoption papers a few years ago. He thought it was better to say T. J. was originally someone else's kid rather than mine. That way no one could trace her to Sarah.

"So once I got the adoption papers, I told T. J. she was adopted. I told her her real family died in a fire. I told her her dad and I were real close. She didn't even question it. She doesn't remember much about her life in Clearwater."

"She didn't even remember me," I said, picking at the tab on my can of Coke. "She said she once had a brother named Sam, but she doesn't remember ever having a sister."

"There was a boy in California she used to play with. His name was Sam, too. Somewhere along the way I think she confused the two of you, and I guess I thought that was okay."

I closed my eyes. Maybe when I opened them I'd find out this whole thing was just a dream. A bad dream.

Unfortunately, it was all real.

"I never stopped thinking about you, Sam," Joe said, his elbows on the table, leaning toward me. "I knew I could never go looking for you. But I always hoped you'd come looking for me. I just didn't think you'd come looking so soon. And I never figured out what I'd do if you actually found me."

"That's why you didn't call me back last week?"

"When I heard that message on the machine, I wanted to take T. J. and run again. But I couldn't do that. My mom—your grandma—she's pretty sick. She's had a couple of strokes and she can't take care of herself anymore. T. J. and me, we're all she has left. She was always there for us, so now it's our turn to be there for her."

I didn't know what to think of this grandmother who had not only abandoned me my whole life, but had helped my dad take T. J. away from us. This grandmother who was probably too sick to explain to me why she'd done it.

"So I had our number changed," Joe went on. "Got it unlisted and hoped that would be enough. After all, it wasn't Suzanne who'd found me, it was you. If you were the one looking for me instead of your mom, I thought maybe you'd just give up. But I bet you're like your mom. You probably never give up."

I couldn't think of many people who would describe me like that.

"I'm nothing like my mom." I always thought I was like him. Casual. Loose. A go-with-the-flow sort of person. But I was different than he was. Very different. I couldn't imagine ever doing what he'd done.

"So, what do we do now?" Joe asked. He looked like an old man and a little kid at the same time.

"I-I don't know." We had to tell my mom. That's what we had to do now.

He slapped his hand down on the kitchen table. "Well, to start with, I guess I should go and get T. J. When we get back, we'll have some supper and then figure out what to do next, okay?"

I nodded. I didn't have a clue what to say. My head was spinning.

Joe squeezed my shoulder and I felt an electric current go right through my skin. It was the first time in ten whole years my dad had touched me. But it was over almost as soon as it began.

"Don't go anywhere," he said as he yanked open the front door. "I'll be back in just a minute."

Chapter Eighteen

I'm not sure how long I sat there at the kitchen table, trying to make sense of everything I'd just heard.

I was so confused. I knew I should probably hate my dad for what he'd done. Thinking about what he did, what he had stolen from Mom and Grandma and Grandpa Sperling and me...it made me feel sick. But for some reason, I didn't hate him. I really didn't. I wasn't sure what I felt for him, but it wasn't hatred.

Then I thought about my mom. What would she do when she found out? She'd have my dad thrown in jail. That much I knew for sure. What he did was a *crime*, right?

T. J. would come live with us and my dad would go to jail and that would be the end of it.

All of a sudden their dog let out a shrill *woof!* His tags jangled as he got up on his hind legs, paws on the front windowsill, tail wagging, and peered out the window.

Were they back?

I got up from the table and went to look outside. Joe and T. J. were sitting on the grass under the big tree. Joe had his arm around T. J. and she had her head resting on his shoulder. Their backs were to me, but because the windows were open I could hear every word they were saying.

"What are we going to do?" T. J. moaned.

"I don't know, honey."

"Will…her mom take me away from you?"

"She'll sure want to try."

T. J.'s shoulders quivered and Joe hugged her tighter to him. "But I want to stay with you," she said. "Can't we run away or something?"

I gasped. T. J. would rather run away with…Joe, who was a liar and a *criminal*, than come live with us?

"You know we can't."

"Because of Grandma, right?"

"Yes."

"I wish she'd never come here!" T. J. cried. Each word she spoke was like a fist in my stomach.

"I wish—"

But I didn't hang around to hear what else T. J. wished. I hustled back to T. J.'s bedroom, where I figured I'd find Angela waiting. We could sneak out the back door, cut across the yards, and be out of here before my dad and T. J. came back. I'd just suck this whole thing up inside me and pretend it never happened. I'd go back home and take whatever punishment my mom wanted to dole out for sneaking off to Minnesota without permission, for sneaking off to the Twin Cities without permission. I'd tell her I didn't know what got into me. I just felt like doing something reckless.

But Angela wasn't in the bedroom.

"Angela?" I called, looking all around.

"In here," she called from a closed door behind me. The bathroom. "I'll be out in a minute."

I sighed, leaning my head against the wall. What was I thinking coming here?

I heard a toilet flush and the water come on. Finally Angela opened the door. "Hey," she said softly. "How'd it go?"

"Fine," I said, grabbing her arm. "But we've got to get out of here. Come on."

"Wait." Angela dug in her heels. "What's the matter, Sam? What happened?"

"This was a mistake," I said. "A huge mistake." I told her a little bit about what my dad had told me and then I told her everything I'd overheard between my dad and T. J.

"I never realized what a mess of things I'd make by coming here," I said. "If my mom finds out about this, my dad will go to jail. And then T. J. will have to come live with us and...she doesn't want to." My throat closed up and my eyes filled with tears. My bottom lip quivered. "Sh-she doesn't even know us, but she doesn't want to live with us." I buried my face in my hands and just let the tears come.

Angela put her arms around me. "Shh," she said, rubbing my back. "I know it hurts, but I have to tell you, Sam, I think I understand how she feels. What if some stranger came along and told you your mom had done something wrong and now you had to go live with him? How would you feel?"

I wiped my tears on the back of my arm and sniffed. "But I'm not just some stranger. I'm her *sister*. Her twin sister."

"You're still a stranger," Angela said.

She was right, of course. And in that instant, I realized that Joe and T. J. were a family, but they weren't *my* family. They were my blood relatives, but they were no more my family than Bob's family was.

I sniffed again. "That's why we have to leave. Now. Before they come back inside."

"No, Sam! You can't just pretend this whole thing never happened. What about your mom? Don't you think she has a right to know the truth?"

Yes, she did. And T. J. and my dad had a right to…to what? I didn't know. I had screwed things up by coming here, and now I didn't know where my loyalties lay. All I knew was I didn't want to be the one responsible for sending my dad to jail. And I didn't want to be the one responsible for ruining everyone's life.

"There's something else you need to know, Sam," Angela said. As if I hadn't already found out enough.

"What?" I asked, slumping against the wall.

"I…talked to your mom—"

"What?" I cried, panic rising in my throat.

Angela led me back to T. J.'s room and we sat back down on her bed. "When I called my dad's house, Noreen answered the phone," Angela explained. "She wanted to know where I was. And then she wanted to know whether you were with me. Your mom was there, Sam. She was at my dad's house. Apparently she drove up to Hill Valley as soon as she got your message this morning."

Oh no. "What did you tell her?"

"I didn't tell her anything," Angela assured me. "Not

about your dad or T. J. I just told her we were at the Mall of America. She wanted to talk to you, but I told her you were in the bathroom. In fact, I've told her that three times now because she keeps calling back. She probably thinks you're sick or something. You're supposed to call her."

"No!" I hurled myself back against the wall. I couldn't talk to my mom. Not yet. What would I say?

"Sam, you have to! She knows something's up, but she doesn't know what. And she and my dad are both on their way to the Mall of America to get us." She checked her watch. "We're supposed to meet them in front of Bloomingdale's in an hour."

"An hour?" I screeched.

Angela nodded miserably. "You've got to call her and tell her where we are."

Or we could just sneak out, run through the backyards, and then cut over to Penn Avenue and catch a bus to the Mall of America. We might even get there before my mom and Angela's dad. Either way, all we'd have to tell them was we felt like sneaking off for a day of fun at the Mall of America. We're teenagers. Teenagers do stuff like that.

No. Angela was right. I had to call my mom and tell her the truth.

I dragged myself to my feet, then tottered over to the window. My dad and T. J. were still out there. I couldn't hear them as well here as I could in the living room, but I didn't want to take any chances on them hearing me. So I took my cell phone into the bathroom and turned on the shower to drown out my voice.

"You're doing the right thing," Angela called over the noise of the water.

I hoped she was right.

I sat down on the toilet seat. Then I opened my purse and took out my cell phone. My whole body was shaking. But one by one I punched in each digit of my mom's cell phone number.

What was I going to say?

Mom picked up on the first ring. "Hello? Sam?"

I gulped. It was so good to hear her voice. "Uh huh."

"Oh, thank God! Do you have any idea, any idea at all, what I've been going through the past twenty-four hours?"

Probably nothing in comparison to what she was about to go through.

"I tell you, Sam, I don't know what goes through your head anymore. I specifically told you to get on that bus this morning and come home, and what do you do? You hop on another bus and take off for the Mall of America? Do you have any idea how dangerous that is?"

"Well—" I began.

"No, you probably don't," Mom went on, her voice rising. If I wasn't careful, I was going to start crying again. "Because you're thirteen and you think you know it all! You think you can do whatever you want. Well, let me tell you something, Sam, there are going to be some changes around here when we get back to Clearwater. Some big changes."

"I'll say," I muttered.

"Are you being fresh with me, young lady?"

"No!" I said right away. Because I really wasn't being fresh. Not this time.

I took a deep breath. "I've got something to tell you, Mom."

"What? What do you have to tell me?"

I glanced over at the stream of water pouring out of the faucet and swirling down the drain.

This was so hard.

"Well," I said weakly. "First I think you'd better pull over. I don't think you should be driving when I say what I have to say—"

"Do you really think I'm driving right now, Samantha?" Mom yelled. *"I am way too upset to be driving!"*

"Oh. Good," I said, relieved. "I mean, good that you're not driving." This was going to come as a huge shock and I didn't want her to drive off the road or anything.

Mom sighed. "What is it, Sam?"

I swallowed again. I wished I could be a little kid again and have her put her arms around me and tell me everything was going to be okay.

"Sam?" Mom said, more worried this time.

There was no easy way to say it. So I just opened my mouth and blurted everything out, "I found my dad and I'm at his house and T. J., I mean Sarah, is here, too. She's alive, just like I thought. And…she's living with him, and…" And I had to stop there because I was out of breath.

But I'd said it.

There was a long pause. Then, "W-what did you say?" Mom asked in a voice barely louder than a whisper.

I closed my eyes and leaned back against the toilet. Did I really have to say it all over again?

"I said, 'I found my dad and—'"

"Sarah's...alive?" Mom interrupted.

"Yes!"

"She's there with you?"

"Well, not right here. She's outside. With him. She didn't know anything about you and me. She thought—well, never mind right now. They're out there talking and then—"

"Where are you right now?" Mom wanted to know.

"I told you, I'm at...my dad's house."

"Yes, but where is that? What's the address?"

I told her.

"You stay put," Mom demanded. "I'm calling the police. I'll be there as soon as I can."

"Wait, Mom! Don't call the police," I begged. What would my dad and T. J. think when the police pulled up in their driveway?

But it was too late. Mom had already hung up.

Chapter Nineteen

I heard the sirens less than five minutes later. Silently Angela and I made our way to the front door. As soon as we stepped outside we saw three police cars pulling up in front of the house.

Joe and T. J. both scrambled to their feet. T. J. turned to me and I saw a look of horror creep across her face.

"You called the police?" T. J. cried with disbelief.

Joe's shoulders slumped. He looked at me with sadness in his eyes.

"No! I just...called my mom—"

"Oh. So *she* called the police," T. J. said in a nasty voice. Which made me kind of mad. I mean, I didn't want my mom to call the police, but I understood why she did. What Joe did was *wrong.* Didn't T. J. see that?

Losing my sister was so painful for my mom that even now, ten years later, she could hardly talk about it. And all along, Sarah—T. J.—was never really dead. It seemed to me that telling people she was dead when she wasn't was one of the worst things he could've done.

I don't know whether I could've said that to T. J. or not, but I didn't even have a chance to try because all those police officers were getting out of their cars and marching over to us. There were six of them—two from each vehicle. A tall female officer told us her name was Detective Becker and she wanted to know which of us girls was Samantha Wright. There was something a little bit freaky about hearing your name come out of a police-woman's mouth. I swallowed hard, then slowly raised my hand.

Then they wanted to know whether my dad was Joseph Wright and whether T. J. was Sarah Wright.

"My name's not Sarah," T. J. said boldly. "It's T. J."

"What's your mother's name, T. J.?" another officer asked.

"I don't have a mother. My mother died when I was little."

"What was her name?" he pressed.

T. J. lowered her eyes. She drew closer to Joe and he hugged her against his chest. I looked away.

"T. J.?" Detective Becker tried to get T. J. to look at her and answer the question, but T. J. just buried her face in my dad's chest.

So the police decided to haul all of us down to the police station.

"You can't do that!" Angela said. "Our parents are picking us up at the Mall of America. They're going to wonder where we are."

"No, I spoke with Sam's mother, and both your parents are planning on picking you up at the police station," Detective Becker explained.

I was surprised how relieved I was to hear that. This whole thing was getting to be too much for me to handle. Way too much. I wanted my mom. And I was willing to let the police take me to her.

But T. J. didn't want to get into that police car for anything. Especially when they told her she was going to ride in one car and Joe was going to ride in another.

"*No!*" T. J. screamed, wide-eyed. She wrapped her entire body around Joe and held on for dear life.

"Please don't make me go!" she cried. "Please!" Tears poured down her face.

Joe was crying, too. His shoulders were heaving and he was clinging to T. J. every bit as hard as she was clinging to him.

It took four police officers to wrestle the two of them apart and drag them into separate vehicles, T. J. kicking and screaming and Joe crying the entire way.

I could hardly bear to watch. This was my sister and my dad. They were both in such pain. And it was all my fault. Well, it was my dad's fault, too, but mostly it was mine. Because I was the one who couldn't leave well enough alone.

Detective Becker led Angela and me to the first vehicle. "You girls can ride with us," she said.

So we crawled into the backseat of the car. I'd never been in a police car before. It smelled bad. Like stale cigarette smoke and cheeseburgers.

There was a glass panel separating the front and back seats, but the officers kept the panel open so they could talk to us. I think they thought we'd feel better if they drove the speed limit and made conversation with us. But the only thing that would make me feel better was if I could go home.

The heavyset guy who was driving had a daughter our age, he told us. She was a swimmer, and I don't remember what else because I wasn't really listening. I just leaned against the window and watched the city go by. And wondered how T. J. was doing in the car behind ours.

When we got to the police station, the officers took us all to separate rooms. They even separated me and Angela. The heavyset guy who drove our vehicle took Angela into one conference room and Detective Becker took me into another across the hall. She flipped a switch and an overhead fluorescent light blinked on.

Detective Becker gestured for me sit down on one of the three chairs surrounding the hard metal table in the middle of the room. There was nothing else in the entire room besides the table and chairs. No books or magazines. Even the walls were bare. There were no pictures. No clock. No outside window. Just a window to the hallway and there were blinds over that.

I chose the closest chair and Detective Becker sat down across from me.

"It sounds like you've had quite a day," she began. "Do you want to tell me about it?"

There was a lot more to tell about than just today, so, once again, I started at the beginning. I told about my visit to the psychic, the newspaper articles, this strong sense I had that my sister was still alive and how I went about trying to find out for sure. I told about how I wasn't supposed to go to Hill Valley with Angela, but that I went anyway, and how this morning I was supposed to get on a bus in Hill Valley and go back home, but instead I took a bus to the Mall of America, and everything that happened after that.

Every now and then Detective Becker wrote something down in her spiral notebook, but mostly she just listened. Then when I finished, we went over it all again so she could make sure she got everything right. Finally she stood up and said she was going to go check on everyone else. And then I was left alone.

I wondered what was going to happen now. They'd probably want to talk to my mom, too, when she got here. Was she here already? Was she in one of the other rooms? What about Angela? Was she still here?

I went to the door, opened it, and poked my head out. Angela and her dad were just coming out of the room across the hall. So my mom *was* here.

"Samantha, hi," Mr. Hunter said all friendly-like, as though we weren't all standing in the middle of a police station.

"Hey, Sam," Angela scurried over and grabbed my hand. "How are you?"

"Okay. Do you know where my mom is?" I asked.

Angela shook her head.

"She and that fellow she came up here with were talking with several police officers when I got here," Mr. Hunter said.

"Fellow she came up here with?" I raised an eyebrow.

"Yes, the fiancé from Iowa—"

Bob? Bob was here, too?

"They came up in their own vehicle," Mr. Hunter continued. "Which was probably a good thing. Sounds like you're all going to be here a while."

I didn't know why my mom had to go and drag Bob along. It wasn't like they were married yet.

"Are you ready to go, Angela?" Mr. Hunter asked.

"In a minute. I just want to say good-bye to Sam first."

Mr. Hunter moved down the hall to give us a little privacy. Once he was far enough away so he couldn't hear, Angela leaned toward me. "Guess what?" she whispered.

"What?"

"My dad thought something bad had happened to us. He was actually *worried.*" She seemed really happy about that.

When I didn't say anything, she said, "Don't you get it? That means *he cares about me.* He even gave me a hug when he saw me. A real hug!"

I smiled. "I'm happy for you, Angela." Really, I was.

"Looks like there's hope for my dad after all. And if there's hope for him, maybe there's hope for your situation, too."

It was weird listening to Angela talk about hope. At the moment, I wasn't sure I'd ever feel hopeful about anything again.

We said our good-byes, then Angela and her dad left. I peered up and down the hallway, wondering where my mom was. Leaving the door slightly ajar, I went back to my seat to wait.

I took out my comb and mindlessly ran it through my hair for something to do. What was happening in all those other rooms? Were my mom and Joe and T. J. giving their own versions of what happened? Were they arresting Joe? Getting T. J. ready to come live with us?

About the time I was starting to think I'd been forgotten, there was a light tapping at my door. I looked up.

"Hey there, Sam," Bob said. Before I even had time to react, he strode right over to me and wrapped his big arms around me.

I just sort of melted into him. Wow. Bob and I had never hugged before. But…it felt okay. Good, even.

"Are you okay?" he asked. There was so much concern on his face that my eyes filled with tears.

"I'll bet you're hungry," he said, handing me a paper bag from McDonald's. Once I saw it, I could smell the hamburger and fries. And then I realized that yes, I was indeed hungry.

"Quarter pounder with cheese, no pickles, right?" Bob asked.

"Yes," I said, surprised that he knew me that well.

"So, what's going on?" I asked. I carried the bag over to the table and took the burger and fries out. "Where's my mom?"

Bob sat down in the chair across from me. "Well, she's talking to some people about what it would take to try and get temporary custody of T. J. tonight, but I don't think she's going to be successful."

"Why not?" I asked, my mouth full of cheeseburger.

"Because this is a very complicated case. It's going to take a while for a judge to talk to everyone and decide what's in the best interests of the child."

"What's complicated about it? My dad committed a crime."

"Well, yes and no," Bob said. "I'm not sure he can really be charged with any crime because at the time he took your sister, there was no divorce. No custody agreement. He had the same rights to you and your sister that your mom had."

What? I swallowed the food in my mouth. "He had a right to tell everyone she was dead and then take her away?" I exclaimed. "He kidnapped her!"

"Not as far as the law is concerned," Bob said. "That's why I'm saying it's complicated."

"But…he lied to the police. He made everyone search the quarry, which must've been really dangerous, not to mention expensive. All for nothing. Isn't that a crime?"

"Well, yes," Bob admitted. "But honestly, we're not likely to do anything about it now. Not after all this time. The real issue here is your sister and what's in her best interest."

I picked at my french fries. "So you don't think Joe will go to jail?" I asked.

"I don't think so. Like I said, the main issue here is going to be custody. And that's going to have to be hashed out in court. The thing is, your sister has been with your dad for ten years. She wants to stay with him. The judge is going to factor that in."

"Have my mom and T. J. seen each other yet?"

"Yes," Bob said. "But it doesn't sound like the meeting went very well. Emotions are running pretty high. On both sides. This is going to take some time."

"Well, if my mom doesn't get custody of T. J. tonight, what will happen to T. J.? Where will she go?"

"I suspect she'll go into temporary foster care."

Foster care? My heart ached for T. J. In foster care, she really would be with strangers.

I suddenly wasn't hungry anymore. "I shouldn't have done this," I said, pushing my half-eaten cheeseburger away. "I shouldn't have gone looking for my dad."

Bob didn't answer right away. "Well, I understand why you did."

I raised my eyes. The main reason I went looking for my dad was I wanted to know what he thought of somebody else adopting me. I wanted him to put his foot down and say no. That he didn't want anyone else to adopt me. That *he* was my dad. How could Bob possibly understand when he was the "somebody else"?

Bob scooted his chair forward a little. "I lost my dad when I was right around your age, Sam. I know what it's like to grow up without a father."

"Your dad got shot on duty, right?" I said slowly. I was pretty sure that was what my mom had said.

"Yes. During a convenience store robbery." Bob had a faraway look in his eyes. "He wasn't the kind of father who spent a lot of time with his kids. He put in a long day at work, came home, and relaxed in front of the television. He was right there in our living room every single night, but I didn't know him. Not really. I didn't know who he was, what he thought about, what he was like as a kid. I didn't even know for sure that he loved me."

It was weird to think of Bob as a thirteen-year-old kid

who just wanted a little love and attention from his dad. Just like me.

"Then when he died," Bob went on, "I realized I'd never know those things. But it was different for you. You didn't know for sure your dad was really gone. You still had a chance to get to know him. That's why you went looking for him. Even though you knew it would hurt your mom."

I swallowed hard. "I never meant to hurt my mom." I never meant to hurt *anybody*. "I just—" How could I justify this?

"You just wanted to know whether your dad could ever love you."

I nodded. Maybe Bob did understand.

"You know, you and I will never be blood relatives." Bob leaned a little closer to me and looked right into my eyes. "But we could still be a family."

I knew that was all he and my mom wanted. For us to be a family. The funny thing was I had been looking for a family, too. Just not the same family my mom and Bob had been looking for. Maybe that was my mistake.

"D-do you have to adopt me for us to be a family?" I asked. I don't know where I got the guts to come right out and ask that question. But that was what it came down to for me. I had nothing against Bob. I just didn't want him to adopt me.

If Bob was upset or hurt, he didn't show it. "A piece of paper doesn't make people a family," he said. "Often family is a choice, not an obligation."

I'd never thought of it that way before. I always knew

you could choose your friends, but not your family. But sometimes you *could* choose your family.

* * *

I yawned. It seemed like Bob and I had been stuck in that little conference room forever. I'd lost track of how many games of hangman we'd played. But we didn't have room on the McDonald's bag for any more games. That was how long we'd been there. I checked my watch. It was almost nine o'clock.

"You getting tired?" Bob asked.

"Yeah, a little," I said. I was getting hungry, too. I wished I hadn't thrown away my cheeseburger.

Bob must have read my mind. He reached into his back pocket and pulled out his wallet. "There's probably a vending machine out there somewhere. Why don't you go get a little snack."

"Okay," I said.

Bob waved a five-dollar bill at me.

"Oh, that's okay. I've got money," I said, patting my purse.

Bob pushed the bill across the table. "Take it," he said. "And while you're at it, bring me some M&M's."

"Okay." I was really in the mood for a bag of M&M's myself. "Thanks."

I went out in the hall. If I went to the left, I knew I'd come out by the front door. I didn't remember seeing a vending machine anywhere that direction, so I went the other way.

The hallway ended at a small waiting room. Two chairs sat on either side of a square table that was piled with magazines. Across the room was a vending machine.

I stopped. T. J. stood in front of the machine dropping coins into the slot.

"I-I didn't know you were still here," I said.

She whirled around when she heard my voice, then slowly turned back to the machine. "I'm waiting for the lady from the Department of Human Services to show up." T. J. pressed a button and her candy dropped to the tray at the bottom.

M&M's.

I leaned against the wall. "My mom's...*fiancé* sent me down here to get us some candy," I said stupidly.

I didn't want her to think I was copying her, so I said, "He wanted some M&M's. I don't know what I'm going to get for myself."

T. J. walked around me without looking at me, then sank down in one of the square chairs. I watched as she ripped open her bag of M&M's.

I didn't know what to do. Should I get what I came here to get and go back to the conference room? Or should I sit down next to T. J.?

I took a good hard look at her, this girl who was my sister. Her eyes drooped and her face was all blotchy like she'd been crying. But her whole life had just been turned upside down, so why wouldn't she cry? And it was all my fault. She must really hate me.

"You probably hate me," T. J. said suddenly.

"What?" Why would I hate her? "I thought *you* hated *me.*"

T. J. blinked. "I don't even know you."

I sat down in the chair next to her, resting one foot under my butt. "I don't know you, either." And I *wanted* to know her. I wanted to know her even more than I wanted to know my dad.

T. J. popped an M&M into her mouth, then offered the bag to me. I shook five candies into my hand, then gave the bag back.

Silence.

"It's not that I don't want to get to know you or your mother," T. J. said after a little while. It sounded weird when she said "your mother." Like my mother wasn't her mother, too. "I just..."

"You don't want to come live with us."

She shook her head and looked down at her lap. "No. I don't want to leave Joe. Or my grandma."

My throat caught when she said that. Her grandma was my grandma, too. And I didn't even know her.

"But Joe took you away from us," I said. "You belong with us."

She shrugged. "He's still my dad. Nothing he did all those years ago changes that. And now your mom wants to take me away from him."

Of course she does. *After what your dad did, why shouldn't she take you away from him?*

"What if it was you?" T. J. asked. "What if you were going on about your life, not knowing anything about me or Joe. And one day Joe just sort of popped into your life and said your mom did something wrong and now you have to come live with us. Would you want to?"

I always thought that if my dad ever came into my life and asked me to come live with him, I'd go in a second. I wouldn't even look back. But would I really? Mom and I didn't always get along, but she was my mom. She was the only parent I'd had. Would I really leave her and go live with some stranger even if he was my dad?

"I don't know," I said truthfully. Maybe I wouldn't.

"I'm still getting used to the idea that I have a mom and a sister. Just because somebody says it's true doesn't make it true. Do you know what I mean?"

I thought about what Bob had said about how a piece of paper doesn't make you family.

I understood T. J.'s point, but still. What about my mom? She wanted her daughter back. Didn't she deserve to have her daughter back?

How would we ever resolve this? There were no right answers. There weren't even any okay answers. No matter what happened, nobody was going to come out of this totally happy.

Chapter Twenty

It was dark outside when we finally left the police station. Bob drove over to a Holiday Inn that was just down the street and he and my mom paid for two adjoining rooms, one for my mom and me and one for Bob.

Mom had picked up my suitcase at Angela's dad's house, but neither of them had bags for themselves. They weren't planning on staying overnight when they left Clearwater this morning. They thought they'd just pick me up in Hill Valley, then go right back home.

"Should we see if we can find a Wal-Mart or someplace where we can get a change of clothes or at least a couple of toothbrushes?" Bob asked as we trudged down the carpeted hallway, looking for our rooms.

"No," Mom said. "I'm tired. We can get something in the morning."

We stopped in front of room 235 and Bob inserted the plastic card in the slot and opened the door. I walked in and plopped my bag on one of the beds. Mom slowly sat down on the edge of the other bed. Bob unlocked the adjoining door between our rooms and went over to check out his room.

"I still think there's something screwy going on here," Mom called to Bob. "Why can't I take Sarah home tonight?"

"T. J.," I corrected. But no one paid any attention to me.

Bob walked back into our room. "Honey, you know why," he said, sitting down with my mom. "A judge is going to have to hear testimony—"

"But why?" My mom sprang to her feet. "She's my daughter! He took my daughter away! And now if she says she wants to stay with him, I may never get her back? It's just not right!"

"No, it's not," Bob agreed.

"There's got to be something we can get him on," she said, stomping around the room. "Falsifying documents? Deprivation of parental rights? Whether we were divorced or not, you cannot tell me that what he did was legal." She glared at Bob as though daring him to contradict her.

"Well—"

My mom cut him off. "What about all the money the county spent on dragging the quarry, looking for Sarah's body all those years ago? Maybe the county can bring charges against him."

"Oh, that'll really make T. J. want to come live with us," I mumbled. "If you find a way to get Joe arrested."

"Sam," Bob said in a warning voice.

Mom whirled around to face me. Her eyes were angry little slits. "Don't call her T. J. Her name is Sarah," she said firmly.

"No it's not!" I stood face to face with my mother. "Sarah is dead. The girl we knew as Sarah is gone. She's never coming back. This girl's name is T. J. We have to call her T. J."

As far as I was concerned, Sarah and T. J. were two totally different people. Sarah was the girl I used to play Barbies with. The girl I once shared a room with. The girl I would've shared all my secrets with, if things had been different. I had no idea who T. J. was. I just knew she wasn't Sarah.

"Your sister's name is Sarah," Mom insisted. We stood eye to eye. Nose to nose. We were so close to one another that I could feel her angry breath on my face. And she could feel mine.

I threw up my hands in frustration. I could not believe the way she was acting.

"Do you really think she's going to want to go back to being called Sarah when she's been T. J. for ten years?" I cried. "Geez, why don't you ever think about what other people want? Do you really think you can control everyone and everything?"

My mom looked like she'd been slapped. But I was just getting warmed up.

I think Bob could tell, too, because he stood up and put his hand on my shoulder. "Now, take it easy there, Sam," he said.

But I couldn't take it easy. I needed to tell my mother how I really felt about some things.

"It's not just T. J., you know. You do this with me, too. You try and control my entire life!"

Mom gasped. "I am your mother! I'm allowed to control your life."

"You shouldn't be allowed to control everything. Did you ever think maybe I needed to know stuff about my dad and my sister? Maybe I don't want to move out of my house and go live in a brand-new house! Maybe I don't want Bob to adopt me!"

"Okay, Sam. That's enough," Mom said. "We're in a hotel here. You cannot carry on like this."

"You're doing it again!" I stomped my foot. "I'm not done talking, but you're still trying to control how much I say!"

I took a deep breath and tried to lower my voice. "Bob and I talked about him adopting me while you were doing whatever it was you were doing at the police station. I told him I wasn't sure I wanted him to adopt me, and do you know what? He's fine with it! You're probably the only one who's going to have a problem with it."

My mom sank to the bed. But I still wasn't finished.

"Haven't you ever heard the phrase: 'If you love something, set it free'? 'If it comes back to you, it's yours. If it doesn't, it never was.' Mom, did it ever occur to you that maybe people don't belong to each other? I don't belong to you! And T. J. doesn't belong to you! If you push this thing with her, you're going to lose her forever! Is that what you want?"

"Whoa!" Bob said, stepping in between the two of us. He made a T with his hands. "Time out. I think the two of you need a break from this conversation. Sam, it's late. Why don't you go to bed."

What? He was telling me when to go to bed?

"And Suzanne…" I realized right then that my mom

wasn't even *looking* at me. "Why don't you come over to my room and we can talk without disturbing Sam."

What *was* she looking at? The wall? She looked like a zombie sitting there. I felt a pain in my chest. Maybe I had gone too far? Or…maybe Bob was right and Mom and I needed a break from this conversation. I was pretty tired.

"Okay, I'll go to bed," I said. I moved my bag so I could pull back my covers.

Bob took my mom's hand and pulled her back up. Then he slowly walked her across the room.

"Good night, Mom," I said quietly. "Good night… Bob."

"Good night, honey," Bob said.

My mom didn't say anything. I wonder if she even heard me.

* * *

I didn't get a lot of sleep that night. I don't think my mom or Bob did, either. All night long I heard muffled voices coming from next door. Sometimes I even heard crying. I didn't think my mom ever cried.

At some point I fell asleep. And obviously my mom must have come back because when I woke up the next morning she was sound asleep in the other bed, her back to me. The door between our room and Bob's was open and I could hear him snoring.

I closed my eyes and tried to go back to sleep, but I couldn't. I was too wired to sleep. What was going to happen today?

A few minutes later I heard my mom roll over. I opened one eye and glanced over at her. She was awake, too.

"Good morning," she said.

I swallowed hard. "Good morning," I said back.

Mom sat up. "I think you and I need to finish our conversation from last night," she said. She sounded a lot calmer this morning.

I was calmer, too. "Okay," I said, pulling my sheet up to my chin.

Mom got up and came over to sit next to me on my bed. I shifted over to make room for her.

"Sam, do you like Bob? Are you okay about us getting married?"

"I like him," I said, gazing up at the sprinkler on the ceiling. "And it's okay that you're getting married." Really, it was. "It's just…it's going to be really different having him in our family, being part of his family, having him live with us."

"Yeah, it will," Mom agreed. She smiled. "But it'll be a good kind of different, don't you think? Bob's a wonderful man. And he loves you as much as he loves me. Believe me, I wouldn't marry anyone who didn't. He wants to be a father to you, Sam."

"I know." I propped myself up on my elbow and looked at my mom. "But Mom, it doesn't matter how wonderful Bob is. I still have another father out there. I know I shouldn't have gone looking for him behind your back. But I just had to know something about him."

"Now you probably know more than you wish you did."

I nodded. "I'm sorry, Mom."

"Me too, honey." Mom leaned over and hugged me. "I wish I had tried harder to find him when you first starting asking questions. I guess I figured once Bob and I were married, Bob would fill that need inside of you. That's why I wanted him to adopt you. But if that's not what you want, that's fine. He and I talked about that last night. He doesn't have to adopt you if that's not what you want."

"I don't know what I want," I said honestly. "I just know there's this hole inside me and I don't know what can fill it. I've known all along that Bob can't fill it. But I don't think that...Joe can fill it, either. It might be that I'm going to need...both Bob and Joe to fill it." I raised my eyebrow, trying to gauge my mom's reaction to that.

But she only flinched a little. "I know you want to get to know your dad now."

I *thought* I still wanted to get to know him. I was still pretty confused about all this.

"I understand that, Sam," Mom said. "Really, I do." She reached for my hand. "It'll take some time, but eventually I'll be at a place where that will be okay."

"Really?" I asked, surprised.

Mom nodded. "As long as you promise to try and be part of your other new family, too. The family that includes Bob and his mother and brother and sisters."

"I can do that," I said. If she could give me the freedom to get to know my dad at some point, then I would do anything for her in return.

Mom scooted back on my bed and leaned against the headboard. "I think the hardest piece of this puzzle is going to be T. J.," she said with a heavy sigh.

I sat up. "Y-you called her T. J.!"

"Yeah," Mom said softly. She put an arm around me. "You were right about that last night."

Mom rested her head against mine. "She goes by T. J. now. We can't go back to calling her Sarah. And if she doesn't want to come live with us, we can't force her to or we'll lose her forever. Just like you said."

"S-so you're not going to try and get custody right now?" I asked.

Mom shook her head. "Bob and I were up most of the night talking about this. Much as I'd like to go in there and demand that T. J. come live with us and Joe go to jail...it just wouldn't be right, would it?"

I looked away. "No, I guess not," I said sadly.

"If she's happy, he must have done something right during these ten years," Mom said.

For a while, neither of us said anything. Then I asked, "Are you glad we found out the truth? Or do you wish we hadn't?"

At first Mom didn't say anything. I could see her weighing it all out in the expressions that passed across her face. Finally she cupped her hand around my chin and smiled. "I think it's always better to know the truth."

"Me too," I said. And then we just hugged each other until Bob came over and asked if it was time for breakfast.

Chapter Twenty-One

Hurry up, Sam!" Mom called from our front door. "We don't want to be late!"

"I'm coming!" I called back. I fluffed my hair a couple more times, then peered at myself in my mirror. My hair wasn't perfect, but it was going to have to do.

I grabbed my purse, then hurried down the hall, weaving through all the boxes. My mom and Bob were getting married in three days. The movers were coming in four days. Grandma and Grandpa Sperling were coming tomorrow. And my sister, T. J., was coming today! I checked my watch. My mom and I had exactly one hour to drive to the Cedar Rapids bus station to meet her bus.

"Do I look okay?" I asked my mom, spinning around for her inspection. I had on a brand-new white seventies-style blouse, my favorite jeans, and a gold monkey necklace.

"You look fine," Mom said. "How do I look?" She was wearing a blue skirt and a button-down white shirt.

"Fine," I said.

Then we went out to the car. We figured that since this

was T. J.'s first visit, Mom and I should go to the bus station to get her alone. T. J. could see Bob later. And she could meet the rest of Bob's family *much* later. Like at the rehearsal dinner. Even Mom realized that all those people might be a little much for T. J.'s first couple of nights here.

My mom had made up the couch in the den for T. J. We decided we'd ask her if she wanted a room at our new house. It would be totally up to her. We all knew she wasn't going to live with us, but she was welcome to visit anytime. For as long as she wanted.

"Are you nervous?" Mom asked as we drove into Cedar Rapids.

"Yes," I said. "Are you?"

"Yes." Mom smiled.

We parked a couple of blocks away from the bus station, then walked back. It was a nice day, so we decided to wait outside.

I checked my watch. Ten minutes. T. J. would be here in ten minutes.

"Do you think she's nervous?" I asked.

"I'm sure she's terrified," Mom answered. "This is a big step for her, coming for the wedding."

T. J. wasn't going to be *in* the wedding like me, she was just coming *for* the wedding. She would be here for one week. And maybe, just maybe, I would go there, to Joe and T. J.'s house for a long weekend in October when we were off from school. Mom was still thinking about that.

"Look! I think this is her bus!" I said as a big bus came around the corner and slowly pulled into the parking lot.

Do You Know the Monkey Man?

As the door to the bus wheezed open, Mom and I grabbed hands. Her hand was just as sweaty as mine.

We watched anxiously as all the people filed off the bus. A woman my mom's age with a little kid, two guys in jeans and T-shirts, an older lady with a flowery dress, and finally...T. J.

She smiled a little when she saw us. She hoisted a medium-sized duffel bag onto her shoulder and walked over to us.

"Hey," she said, stopping in front of me.

"Hey," I said back.

It wasn't much, but it was a start.

About the Author

DORI HILLESTAD BUTLER is the author of many works of fiction and nonfiction for young readers. Her middle grade novel SLIDING INTO HOME has received numerous awards, including an Honor Book Award from the Society of School Librarians International. Butler lives in Coralville, Iowa, with her husband, two sons, a dog, a cat, and a fish named Willie, who keeps her company while she writes. Visit Dori Hillestad Butler's website at *www.kidswriter.com.*